Tolle Lege is a Latin phrase commonly associated with St. Augustine and chosen many years ago as our school motto. Originally referring to the Bible, it means, 'Pick up this book and read.'

TOLLE LEGE

# Tolle Lege II

**Written, illustrated, edited, designed, typeset, published, marketed and distributed by the Pupils of St. Augustine's Primary School, Coatbridge.**

First published in 2022 by
Jam Neck II,
c/o St. Augustine's Primary School,
Henderson Street,
Coatbridge,
North Lanarkshire,
Scotland ML5 1BL

in association with
Jam Jar Lurker & Son.

The moral right of the authors and artists has been asserted.
A CIP catalogue record for this book is available from the
British Library.

Paperback: ISBN 978-0-9538806-3-8
eBook: ISBN 978-0-9538806-4-5

Digitally mastered by Francis O'Dowd in the cupboard under the stairs.
Printed and bound by Printondemand Worldwide, Peterborough.

# Contents

**Front Cover** ~ *Ciara Mullen*
**Back Cover** ~ *text by Rosa Cummings;*
*artwork by Kai Williams & Orlaith Higgins*
**2004 Jam Neck Logo** ~ *Rachael Maxwell*
**2022 Jam Neck II Makeover** ~ *Lucy Fern*

# Preface
## by Caroline Docherty
### Headteacher of St. Augustine's.

The written word is a powerful tool that can tell a story, share a message, encapsulate an emotion and record our hopes and dreams at any given moment in time. It has the power to do many things and our 2022 Book Project has provided the perfect platform for our pupils to share their imagination, their hopes and dreams, their fears and their wishes for the future. I am delighted that the entries submitted and published for your enjoyment give a flavour of the world our children inhabit. It provides a perfect snapshot of life in 2022. What an unprecedented few years we have all experienced. Our children have shared these strange times with us when they were so much talk of a worldwide pandemic and yet the things that are important to them remain family, friendships and that sense of belonging.

Many years ago, the school compiled an anthology of pupil writing thanks to the great work of Mr O'Dowd. Now, some 18 years later and once again thanks to Mr O'Dowd, we see how our children view their world and what is important to them. In essence nothing has changed. Children are children and have childlike thoughts and aspirations and that is the way it should be. However, they must grow up in a world vastly different from our own childhood and they are making a fine job of it and doing it with great insight and wisdom. They really are a credit to us all.

It has been an absolute pleasure to read the anthology and be captivated by the innocence of youth. Long may it continue.

Caroline Docherty

Proud Head Teacher

# Foreword
## by Lewis Capaldi

**Scottish singer-songwriter whose debut album was the bestselling record in the UK for both 2019 & 2020, and whose single 'Someone You Loved' has become the longest-running top 10 UK single of all time by a British artist.**

Hi Lewis Capaldi here!

Just wanted to say well done to everyone who took part in creating this book. Never stop writing. Write about everything. Write about your family, friends, memories, feelings. Then one day you can turn them all into songs and be as famous as me :)

All the love

*[signature]*

# Introduction
## by the Jam Neck II Editorial Team

*We have made an excellent book*
*That you should buy and take a look,*
*Flip the pages and you will find,*
*Stories and poems that will blow your mind,*
*So pick it up and take a look*
*At our very magnificent book.*

~

We would like to thank
Lewis Capaldi, Dani Capaldi, Amanda O'Dowd,
everyone who contributed a story, poem or drawing,
the Staff of St. Augustine's,
everyone who pre-ordered the book,
and all the companies who generously sponsored us.

Grace Haggerty   Liam Herlihy  Joe Potter
Mikee McKay  Gilbert hagerty
Grace Hyland (11  Suzie Wilks   Grace Gaffney
Maya Ferguson   Emily O'Donnell   Aarran Innes

# Prologue

Lucy Fern

# When the World Closed Down
## by Suzie Wilks

There was once a time
When the world closed down,
When everyone's face wore
A permanent frown.

There was once a time
When the world just stopped,
A time when everyone
Wanted to be dropped.

But that was a time
When the world was in danger,
When we thought our friends
Were strangers.

But thanks to the pandemic
Some have become more athletic,
And maybe even
Academic.

Thankfully the world
Has been renewed,
And now many more dreams
Can once again be pursued.

# Primary 1

School
Shop

Theo Wallace Clark

i LIRE spedis.

**Ander Orellana**

I liRe going to the cinema with my family and my friends.

**Beth Cummings**

I like to play football
and score goals with
my cousin.

Blake Dornan

I went to the canakan in the summer It was good.

Cairo Ahmed

I ilk to pay
in my house
with
my dad.

Caleb Pirie

I like to got oth my brothers

**Chay McKay**

I like to play
with my dad.
We play football.
My favourite
thing is scorchg
gols.

I like to go to the
Park with my mum.

**Elias Rodgers**

I Love my
big brother. We
Like to play
with my toys.

**Emma Hart**

I Like to go to the swimming with my friend Emma.

**Isla Burns**

I like to go to the swimming with my mum.

Isla Halpin

I like to get a present on my birthday.

Lauren Currie

± L o

f

o

L o g a n

Logan Lawson

I love toplay
in the garden.
on my trampoline.

**Millie Harris**

I Like to Play
Fortnite with my
big brother.

Nathan Rea

I like to pray th the park with blake. we play br the swings.

Noah McLaughlan

My favourite thing to
do is   play  with my
friends.

**Orlagh Reilly**

I li ke to play on rope.
I like to play with my
car.

PJ Chapman

'I like to play at my friends house.

**Rose O'Neill**

I Love to Play Fornite with My dad

Theo Wallace Clark

I like to get
presents on my
birthday.

Vivienne Travers

I like to play with Nathanael.

**Charlotte O'Dowd**

I like to Pley
Bingo With my
brother

**Grace Travers**

I liRe to playWith
my PLaysticoh.

Jack Park

I like to go to a

restaurant with
my family.

**James Drummond**

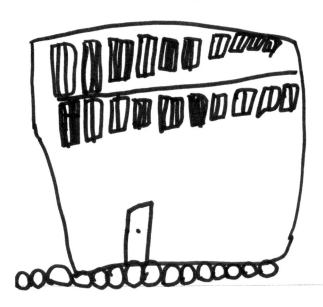

I LIKE to go to the caravan with my family.

**Katie Roy**

I like to play
with my dog.

Mairead Nelson

I like to play with my dog Paddy.

Morven Clark

Nathan Michalak

I like to stay in the garden.

Oliver Thompson

I like to play football

**Vincent Mullen**

I like to play
football.

Lewis Linnen

I like to draw and paint.

**Murron Kerr**

I like to play board games with Nathan.

Adam Mai

I love to play in the snow with my uncles.

**Conlan-Liam Bree**

I like going to swimming.

**Daria Spence**

I like to watch my tablet and my Tv.

Esmae Boyd

I LiKe to PLAY WiTh my dog in the garden

**Georgia McMahon**

I LiKe to play wit my dog in my house.

Leah McAuley

I like to go to the park
With my friends.

**Lilah Tierney**

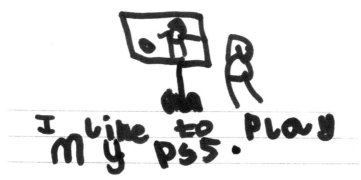

I'm like to play my PS5.

## Luca Tierney

I like to Play foot ball.

**Quinlin Hill**

I like To go To gym nas tics.

**Summer Allison-Smith**

# Monster Truck
## by Tom Madden

Once I had a monster truck. I cut my foot, so I had to stay still. I was stuck and thought I would have to cook and eat my foot.

But then I saw something.

I saw a zombie behind me. It was so scary.

On the other side of me was a ghost.

I got a fright. But then I remembered you can drive through a ghost.

# Me, Little Ladybird
## by Rachel Kirkland

Hi, I'm Little Ladybird. I have so much fun with my friends. I'll tell you about them.

One is Ant.

She is my best friend. We go to school together. One day at school we got a prize.

Now I'll tell you about the day we had a sleepover. It was so cool. So I'll tell you about it. We went home from school and said to our mums, 'Can we have a sleepover?'

And they said, 'Yes, you can.'

Then that day Ant came to my house. We had a lot of chocolate. Then we played hide and seek. It was so fun. My mum said we should watch a movie, so we did; Toy Story 4. And we had some more chocolate.

Then my Mum said, 'It is dinner.' She got pizza! We love pizza. It was so good.

Then we had ice cream. Yum.

Then we had to go to bed.

# Ben's Amazing Day
## by Arnold Hagerty

There lived a boy called Ben. Ben lived with his mum and dad. His neighbour Jack was his best friend. His other neighbour was his gran. Everyday Ben and Jack would go to school. The school was about fifteen minutes away.

When Ben got to school he did maths and division. He got a big prize because he was very good at it. He learned arrays and did division in arrays.

After school Jack stayed till dinner and had hot dogs and watched Hotel Transylvania at Ben's house. Then Jack went back to his own house.

And that was Ben's amazing day.


# Queen Marshmallow
## by Asha Kunderan

At the start there was an alien. She lived on the planet Marshmallow.

Many days later the planet blew up and she was the only alien left, so she went to Earth.

Nobody liked her, so she went back to space.

She found another planet where everybody loved her. She even became the Queen.

# The Mysterious Robot
## by Daniel Gallagher

Once upon a time there was a robot. He and his owner enjoyed having fun together. The robot liked to whiz around the house. The robot had a mysterious secret. It was a flying power! He never told his owner that he knew how to fly.

The robot went to school. On his first day he learned how to write. At break he accidently took his jotter outside! He had to take his jotter back in. Then he got caught and went in detention!

When he went in detention he tried to escape. Then suddenly he saw a rope. He pulled it and it let him go out. When he climbed out, he went to class. He made new friends. Then finally he did some maths.

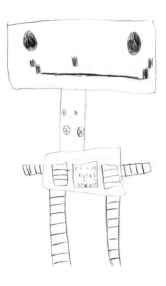

# The Fairy that Liked to Go on Adventures
## by Amelia Kane

Once upon a time there was a little fairy called Emily. She lived in Fairyville. She had lots of brothers and sisters. She had a big mouse that took her anywhere she wanted to go. She was very kind to others.

Her dad trusted her to do anything. He was always being very kind to his daughter. When she was seven she was allowed to hunt in the forest for food.

When she was in the forest she met a bear and it was very kind. Emily the fairy was very caring and loving to animals. She was kind to her brothers and sisters.

And they lived happily ever after.

# Matt's Excellent Day
## by Aedan Rybak

Matt was a very nice boy. He was so nice, his dad said, 'We can go bowling.' So they did.

On the way there they got lunch because it was on the way. Matt had a burger. Matt's dad also had a burger.

Ten minutes later they got to the bowling. Mat got one hundred and one. Matt's dad got one hundred and twenty.

# The Little People
## by Ruary McDines

One upon a time there were tons of little people three apples high. They lived in mushrooms.

One night they were sleeping and one of them was having a bad dream.

She woke up and it was her birthday.

Her friends gave her a surprise party. They went to New York and met some more friends.

Then they went to a forest and this is how they got there: they met an enormous snake thing; they had to go on some boats; and then they had to go underground.

Dear Mum and Dad,

I am writing to ask if I could please get a pet giraffe. I know it sound strange but I have some very good reasons. I know a giraffe would be a great pet for me.

The first reason is you can use it to cut the grass for you!

The second reason is me and my friends can use it for a slide for the trampoline.

The third reason is it can cut down the trees if they are too tall.

The fourth reason is the giraffe can play with you if you are bored.

The fifth reason is that it can take me to school if you want a lie in.

The sixth reason I will feed it and give it water to drink.

The seventh reason is I would take care of it a lot.

The eighth reason I would take it for some walks in the street.

The ninth reason is if the ball goes over to Sofia's house, it could get it.

Your loving daughter,

Olivia Lee

# My Rhyme
## by Grace Rooney

The cat
Sat on the mat,
Wearing a hat,
Watching a bat
Chase a rat.

# Sally's Lucky Day
## by Orla McPhillips

Once upon a time there was a little girl called Sally. She was six years old and it was her lucky day. She got marshmallows for breakfast.

After breakfast Sally went a walk in the park. She found two talking trees. One was called Henry, and the other was called Zoozey. One was grumpy; the other one nice. They became friends, but the grumpy one wasn't sure about that.

Sally arrived home. She had lollipops for lunch. She went out to play. When she went home she had dinner. She had ice cream for dinner.

And that was Sally's lucky day.

# The Pencil and the Glue Stick
## by Italiah Landles

Once upon a time lived a pencil and a glue stick.

The pencil wanted a friend because it was lonely.

So the pencil went to the park and the pencil met a glue stick. Then they became friends. They were BFFs.

They went to the glue stick's house. They played games, then they had a sleepover.

Then the next morning they got breakfast. They got pancakes.

They said, 'Yum yum.'

# The Haunted House
## by Leo Priesty

One day me and my cousin Orla were at a high school disco. But we accidently took the wrong road and ended up at a haunted house!

'Hello', I said. It was creepy and horrifying. We were scared. The lights went on and off, and a ghost was moving.

We ran into the science lab but Frankenstein saw us.

'Ah! Run!' We screamed.

We saw a zombie.

Finally, we jumped in our car and we drove home to our houses.

'Phew,' I said.

# The Dogs and the Bird
## by Hannah Clark

Once upon a time there was a happy dog called Paddy. He had a white bit of fluff on his tummy and the rest of him was black. Paddy's friend was a budgie called Pepe. Pepe loved to ride on Paddy's back in the house and Paddy loved it because Pepe massaged his back with his feet.

They had friends called Snowball and Snowy. They were Westies and they loved to chase Pepe. But Pepe was always flying too high. One day they could not find Pepe because he flew upstairs and he was hiding.

So Paddy went looking for him.

When Paddy found him, Pepe was jumping from Snowball's back to Snowy's back and giving them a massage. They loved it. When Pepe saw Paddy he flew on to his back and gave him a massage.

Everybody had a good day.

# Something in the Forest
## by Gracie McAdam

Once upon a time a little girl went for a walk, and she passed a forest, and she went in.

'Let's go in the forest!' the girl said.

She went in and she heard a big bang! She thought nothing of it. She kept on walking. She heard something. It was someone shouting, 'Help! Help!' She followed the sound, and it took her a long time.

She said, 'Hello, is someone there?'

Someone said, 'Hello!'

She said, 'Who are you?'

Someone said, 'I can't tell you, but I am coming for you.'

The girl got scared, she started to run. The person started to chase her. The girl was screaming. The person caught her.

The girl shouted, 'HELP! HELP! SOMEONE!'

But nobody heard her, and she was never seen again.

# Jack's First Day at School
## by Ciaran McHugh

There lived a boy called Jack. He was five years old.

On Monday it was his first day at school. He was very nervous.

He made four friends: Luke, JoJo, Anton and Julie.

They gave him confidence in his maths, in reading, in science and in English.

He had fun.

Ciaran McHugh

Seren Robertson

Zack Hay

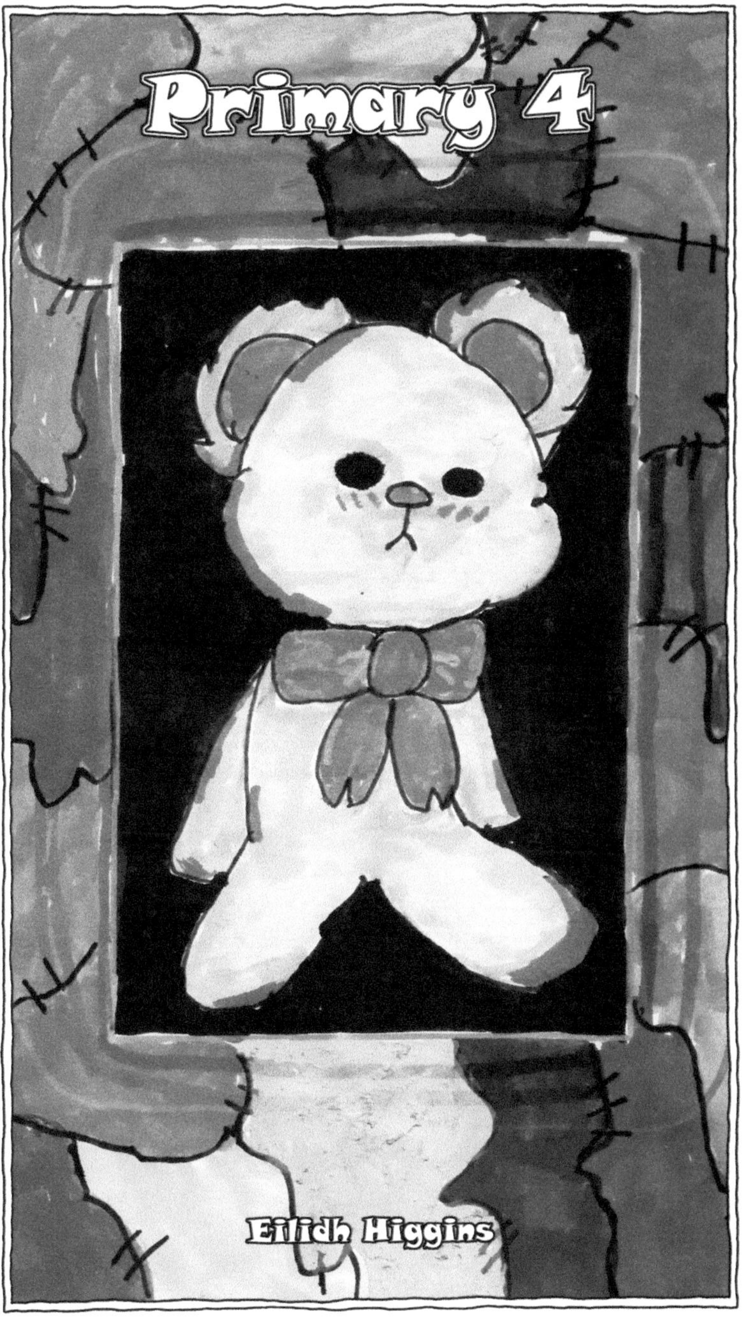
Primary 4
Eilidh Higgins

# Anna and the Orphanage Kids
## by Sophia Currie

Once upon a time there was a girl called Anna. Anna was nine years old. Anna had friends called Annie, Sophia, Connie and Belle. Anna had jobs because the orphanage ladies were poor. Her friends had jobs too, but not a lot because Anna was the oldest.

'I'm going to get some food,' said Anna and she went to get food for all the people from the orphanage.

Now to tell you more about the ladies who took care of the kids. They were called Nora and Laya.

One day Connie said to all of her friends, 'We should escape. I'm bored here.'

'Well, I don't think we should,' said Anna.

'But why?' asked Connie.

'Because the ladies will be sad. Plus, we won't have anywhere to stay.'

'Or will we?' replied Connie.

'Fine,' said Anna. 'Let's go.'

Anna, Annie, Sophia, Connie and Belle climbed up to the roof of the orphanage. Anna saw ropes to get down, so they swung off the roof and landed outside the orphanage. They ran all the way to the city.

'Ugh!' said Anna. 'We really should not have come here. It's so cold.' The friends explored the city looking for kind people who could accept them into their house. 'Connie, we're never going to find any people. Plus, what we are doing is very dangerous.'

Anna and her friends searched everywhere, but none of the citizens were able to keep five children forever.

The next day, Nora and Laya searched for the children. They found them looking at the homes. Nora and Laya knew what they were doing. They showed the children a house.

'They will accept you,' Nora said.

Living in the house was someone who wanted five kids. 'Hi,' she said. 'Come with me.'

Anna and her friends lived happily in their new house.

# The Little Tiger and the Liger
## by Scarlett Cairns and Caoimhe Cox

Hi. My name is Little Liger. If you are wondering why I have a weird name, it's because my dad's a lion and my mum's a tiger. I get *Li* from my dad (because *Li* is at the start of lion). And I get *ger* from my mum (because *ger* is at the end of tiger).

I love my family. I love my dad because, well, I do. And I love my mum because she gives me great big hugs.

My mum has been deciding if she should adopt a half price tiger who is five months old. She wants to do this because, well, she's never had a baby tiger. She's only had a baby liger (me) and she's a tiger. So she wants to see what it's like having a baby tiger. So… well, yeah.

Anyway, soon it's my birthday and that means lots of **TOYS**. But I'm worried in case my mum buys me the five month old tiger. My dad says she's not buying me the five month old tiger. But I'm still worried because on my last birthday I asked my dad if my mum was getting me some slime. And he said no. But in the end my mum did get me some slime.

Anyway, I don't care if my mum adopts the five month old tiger because I'm lucky to have a family. Not everyone does.

## Summer
## by Belle O'Donohue

The sun is on the sand,
Burning my little hand.

The sun is on the sea,
Oh, it's blinding me!

Digging with my spade,
I must stay in the shade.

It's good to be in Rome,
Instead of heading home.

# Kylie and Rachel
## by Orlaith McDonagh

Kylie and Rachel were best friends forever. They lived in a village called Rise. It was an enchanted village.

Kylie and Rachel went to the park one day. Kylie's dad and Rachel's mum came too. There was a strange looking man at the park. Kylie and Rachel were scared of him. He was very old and wore old clothes. He wore a black leather jacket.

Kylie and Rachel knew the man lived on the hill and decided to find out more about him. When he left the park, they followed him. They decided to sneak away from their parents. They followed behind the man up the hill.

From the outside the house looked very creepy and dark. The girls went to the back of the house. They were amazed.

The garden was beautiful. It had rainbow stairs and lots of flowers. They walked up the rainbow stairs and into the house. They couldn't believe their eyes. It was the nicest, most magical house ever.

The living room was upside down. The furniture was on the ceiling and the lights on the floor. The girls walked through to another room that had ice statues. This was the best house ever.

Kylie walked by the statues and into another room. It was like a garden inside. There were pebbles;

all different colours. Kylie ran over to them and picked one up. There was a bright light and then silence. Rachel ran over and screamed. Kylie was frozen. Rachel didn't know what to do.

The old man heard Rachel's scream and came into the room. He was surprised to see the girls. Rachel shouted at him to help. The man walked over. He looked different to when they had seen him at the park. He was young now and had a bright pink jumper on.

He leaned over and put his hand on Kylie's head. Kylie screamed. She wasn't frozen anymore. She ran to Rachel and hugged her.

Rachel thanked the man. He said it was okay but asked why they had followed him. The girls said sorry, but they had wanted to see what his house was like.

Rachel asked if he lived on his own. He said yes. Kylie asked if he had any friends. He said no. Kylie and Rachel felt sorry for the man. They asked his name. He told them Alex.

Rachel asked if they could be friends with him. Alex said he would like that; he was lonely in this big house.

The girls heard their parents shout their names. They told Alex they had to go but he could come to the park with them and their parents tomorrow. Alex said he would like that. He didn't look old anymore and the house didn't seem creepy from the outside anymore.

Alex, Kylie and Rachel became great friends and had great fun playing in the amazing magic house on the hill.

# Best Friends Break Up
## by Kaiya McLorinan

There were two best friends. One was called Olivia and the other was called Gracie. One day they were playing tig at the park and Olivia accidentally pushed Gracie onto the road.

Thankfully there were no cars coming.

But Gracie was still very upset. I would be.

Olivia tried to phone Gracie. She tried again. There was no answer. She walked home. But she saw a house with Gracie's name on it. Olivia walked in.

There Gracie was.

'Hi,' Gracie said.

Olivia asked, 'Why are you so upset?'

'I'm not,' said Gracie. 'I was wondering how long it would take.'

'What do you mean?' Olivia said.

'It's all a big prank.'

'What?' Olivia said, being very confused.

'I love you so much. Let's go check out this house.' said Grace. 'It's fine; you will not get hurt.'

'Are you sure?'

'Yes.' Said Gracie. 'Let's go into that bedroom, it's not scary.'

**SOMETHING HAPPENED!**

*To be continued…*

# Bob the Blob's Adventure
## by Orlaith Burns and Eilidh Higgins

Once upon a time there was a blob and his name was Bob. He was very nice and played with his friends until one day a new game came out. Then all he did was sit in his room and play the game.

One day Bob's game started to *bleep*. Then his hand was not there! Then before he knew it, he was in his game!

So he was in the game and a voice said, 'Welcome Bob, you are in Candyland. Now you have to escape. You will find clues along the way.'

Bob was scared.

Bob saw the first level. It was lollipops. He had to jump over them or else he would fall into sticky jelly. But he got on to Level Two.

'Yay!' he said.

Then he got to Level Two and he just kept falling and falling.

Then somehow he was on Level Three. It was the final level and it was a big one: *Hide and Seek.* For this round Bob could shapeshift. There was a seeker. Bob had to hide. If the seeker did not find him in 5 minutes, Bob would escape. Then it had been 5 minutes.

Bob was home safe. He said sorry to his friends and they all lived happily ever after.

Luke Copland

James Hyland

Belle O'Donohue

# The Four Boys at St Augustine's
## by Drew Hanlon, Jack Hendry,
## Rory Moore and Harrison Rea.

Once upon a time, there was a group of boys that never left each other, even at the summer holiday. They would play Fortnite every night. When the summer holiday finished, they would run up and hug each other.

When school started, if one got stuck they would help each other, even if they would get in trouble.

When it was Thursday they played football. And because they were best friends, they would help each other.

Chris Hanlon

# Hazel's Horror
## by Naomi Kirkland

Hazel was walking home from school one dark winter's night. It was cold and Hazel was shivering, but she kept walking.

'Ow!' Hazel called. She had tripped over a big jaggy stone. Then, out of the corner of her eye she saw a house. Not just an ordinary house; a dark, gloomy house. The only light was from a small window in the attic. Hazel thought for a moment. Should she go into the house or head home to have her mum's disgusting homemade soup? If she went into the house she could warm up. So that's what she decided.

As she got nearer it got darker and darker until finally she reached the door. It creaked open. Hazel stepped in very slowly and the **BANG!** The door slammed behind her!

Hazel ran back to the door and to her surprise it was locked. She started to panic. It was so dark. She started feeling for a light switch until she found one…

She saw she was in a lovely big house with big velvet stairs. Maybe it was just the outside of the house that was creepy? The Hazel heard a voice saying, 'Who's there?' She ran to hide behind a big box. Someone was coming down the stairs and then…

**Ding ding!** Hazel's alarm went off.

'Phew!' Hazel sighed. 'It was just a dream!'

# Doggy Life
## by Cara Lochran

Hi, my name is Cooper. I woke up on a Friday morning and I was very excited and happy because it was the last day of my mum having to go to school for the week. I ran into my mum's room to wake her up because I was so excited for my morning cuddles. I jumped on her and she was very happy to see me.

We cuddled for around half an hour, then my mum had to get out of bed and I was sad. So she decided to give me my favourite treats. Then I decided to leave her alone to get dressed while I was eating my treat. Once she was dressed, she went downstairs to get breakfast. She also gave me some breakfast. My mum had toast and I had some biscuits.

Once we had finished eating my mum had to get ready to leave for school. I got really sad and started to cry. I got distracted and my mum left the house. I got really sad. Until about five to ten minutes later when my pappa came. I did not know what was happening. Then he lifted me up and put me in the car and started to drive. Then I realised where we were going. We were going to my gran's house. I got really excited because my gran has a dog called Sooty and Sooty is my best friend.

When we finally arrived, I was excited to get out the car. My pappa lifted me out and put me on the ground and I ran up to the door. I couldn't wait to get in but my papa was taking **AGES**. When he finally got his keys, after what felt like eighty-four years, he opened the door. I ran in full of excitement. Then my gran was very happy to see me, so I did not know who to go to or what to do. So, I played with Sooty for around fifteen minutes then went to see my gran.

My pappa brought my gran food but I got jealous and sat on my gran's knee so she could not eat it. I wanted Sooty and I to share it instead. My pappa brought me and Sooty treats so I would come off my gran's knee. Around thirty to forty minutes later my mum came in from school. I was really happy to see her. I jumped up on the couch. She gave me a cuddle. I liked it because it felt very good. Then after a little while my pappa offered my mum some dinner. My mum said, 'Yes.' I was happy because that meant I had more time to play with Sooty. Although after my mum had finished, we had to leave, and I was sad. But I knew I would then get to play with my mum anyway, so we left.

Once we got home it was around 7:00pm. We were quite tired, so we watched a movie called Dennis the Menace. It was on for around one hour and thirty minutes. It was very good. When it was finished it was around 8:30pm. I got some biscuits again. Then we went upstairs and got ready for bed. I do have my own bed, but I just sleep in my mum's instead. Once we were ready for bed we then lay down and cuddled for about thirty minutes. Then went to bed. The next day, when I woke up my mum wasn't there. I got a bit worried then heard a noise downstairs. I went to look, and it was Mum making us breakfast. I had some cocktail sausages and some ham. My mum had some boiled eggs and toast. Today was my favourite day because it was Saturday! It was my favourite day because my mum doesn't go to school. So we got a day in the house together. Oh, and did you know? I have four paws and I am a Cavalier King Charles Spaniel puppy.

# Village Girl's Diary
## by Aoife Doran

### Monday 16th April 2018

Oh no! I haven't woken up to my alarm and I am not going to get people's newspapers on their doorsteps on time. What am I going to do? I need to get ready like lightning and hopefully I'll make it on time. I'm so confused why my alarm didn't work this morning.

### Thursday 19th April 2018

A few days ago, a mysterious invite appeared at my door. I was confused as I didn't have any idea what it was about. I opened it up with excitement as Mum and Dad sat on the sofa with a cup of tea. I read it aloud so they could hear. I was delighted to discover that the village were hosting a party to celebrate all the amazing work in the village and what we have achieved. I was so excited. Thoughts of what will I wear and who else will be there filled my head.

## Saturday 28th April

At last, the day of the village party has finally arrived. It's half past four and I have half an hour until the big event. I can't even explain how excited I am. I think our village really deserves this as we have all worked hard and put in our own bit to making this village be our home. Anyway, I have been talking far too much. I can't believe it's only ten minutes until the big event. Mum and Dad are calling me, so I have to go...

## Sunday 29th April 2018

The party has finished but I wanted to tell you about my spectacular night. I had a blast tonight. It felt extremely weird because my usual routine was different. I didn't have to collect the dinner from the shop, or tidy my bedroom. But I must admit, I really enjoyed doing something a little different. The full village were up and dancing all night. Laughter and happiness filled the village streets. I will remember this special night forever!

# A Day I Will Never Forget
## by Claudia Martin

Hello. My name is Lilly. I am sixteen years old. On the day before my birthday, my family and I were on holiday. It was the summer holidays and we wanted to get away for some time. We had been away for five days so far, and still had four more days to go.

The first thing we did on that day was to get ready and go to the beach. Only me and my four year old sister went because my parents were going to the shops. When we got to the beach we went straight into the sea. After that we went home because it was 8 pm and we had been there a while. When we got in the house we got pizza. Then we all went to bed.

*Ring! Ring!* The alarm went off. It was my **BIRTHDAY!!!** I got out of bed and went to see my family.

'Hi Mum, Dad and Lucy!' I squealed. 'I am so excited to open my presents. Can I open them right now?'

'Yes, of course.'

'Okay! This one first. Yeah, it's the phone case I wanted. Thank you, I love it. Now, this blue one… Is it new clothes? Let's open my two cards. £40 altogether; that's a lot. Now that last one. OMG! Grandma's necklace! Thank you so, so much. This is my favourite present of all. I am always going to wear this. I am even going to put it on right now!'

The next day, four of my friends and I went to the beach to chill out. We had food, drinks, balls; everything. All of us were sunbathing. Then we decided we would go in the sea for a while. We were all having so much fun. It was the best day of my life. After playing volleyball, we went to lie down.

Suddenly I noticed my necklace was gone!

My heart was racing. I was so worried. This was not like any other necklace. It was my grandma's and she had worn it every single day. Before she died, she said she would give the necklace to me some special day. We all looked everywhere but we couldn't find it anywhere. I saw a guy with a metal detector and asked if we could borrow it. Thankfully he said yes. It was buzzing so much but we still didn't have any luck. We looked at one more space… and there it was! I was so happy. If we hadn't looked there, it would have been gone forever because it was right next to the sea.

I was so relieved. I just wanted to go back to the hotel and put my necklace in a safe place. That evening I was lying in bed and I kept looking at the necklace. It was shining so bright, like the brightest star in the night sky. I believe this was my grandma smiling back at me. This day I will never forget.

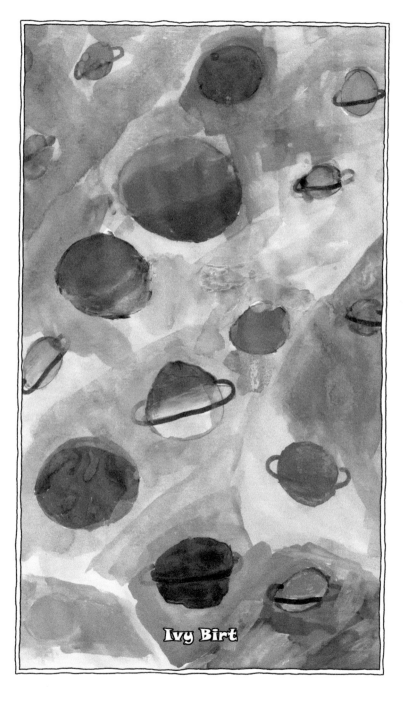

Ivy Birt

Aoife Doran

# A Boat to Australia
## by Erin McDonagh

There was a girl who took the boat to Australia. She was going to visit her mother and father. The girl was called Gemma. She had to take the boat because aeroplanes were delayed and she couldn't wait to get there.

On the boat, Gemma took her car and parked it underneath with the other cars. The boat was super big and had lots of amazing things onboard. Gemma's favourites were the cakes and the jelly they served. The boat was super fast, faster than Gemma ever thought it could be. It felt like they had magic powers and were flying faster than any plane could. She was sad to get off the boat, but when she saw her mother and father she was so happy. Her brother and sister were there too.

Gemma's favourite thing to do with her family was to eat breakfast. Her mum made the best pancakes and toast. Gemma enjoyed lots of days out with her family. They had lunch in lovely places and ate lovely things. They saw lots of snakes and Koala bear on their travels. Gemma's favourite animal was the kangaroo.

She visited lovely places and saw some amazing things. Her favourite was the Sydney Harbour Bridge. Gemma's visit went by quickly and before she knew it, she had to go back home. But her mum and dad had a surprise for her: they were coming to live with her!

Gemma was very happy. She loved her visit to Australia and loved getting the boat back home with her parents.

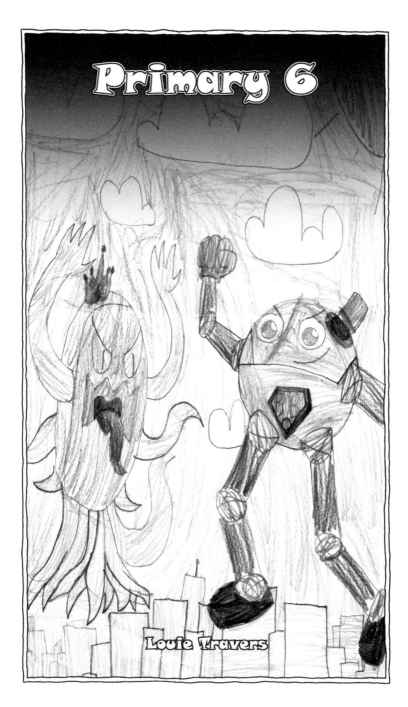

# The Tentabot
## by Leo McGinness

Hidden away from the energetic city, in a nondescript town, an evil cabal of scientists were conspiring to create the robot menace of the future. They had been experimenting for seven months using DNA from an octopus, a shark and the venom from a viper. Suddenly, just as the scientists were returning from lunch, *BANG!* The tests fail and a gruesome, hideous creature arises named the **Tentabot!**

Terrorising the streets by launching cars mercilessly, the Tentabot obliterates everything in its path. House by house, building by building, it has crushed the whole town in hours, but it is hungry for more. First towns, then countries, then **CONTINENTS,** and it's not showing any signs of stopping…

# The Old Wood
## by Grace Hyland

The spooky silence is deafening; it rings in your ears. The only light is from the glowing full moon. When a cloud drifts across it, all is pitch black.

Pattering feet rustle the dead leaves on the forest floor. Ancient old trees that had long since fallen block the path. Your feet sink into the springy green moss.

Twisted trees rise on either side of you. Fungi in odd colours sticking to their long, rotten, leafless branches.

The glow of yellow eyes watching you, ready to pounce or to flee.

Unease floods your brain like an icy cold wave. Your feet take over and continue to walk forwards, deeper into the woods. Your body and mind are screaming to turn back, to go home.

It isn't cold but you shiver as the breeze blows over your body. Bursts of colour come from clumps of toadstools at the roots of the magnificent trees.

The old wood stretches for miles in every direction.

Many people are lost in the wood but, if you are lucky enough, you will make it out of the creepy forest.

Just like me.

I would advise you only to go to the old wood if you have a map.

# The Dragon of Doom
## by Brendan Hughes

One stormy morning as all the kids went to school, little did they know something terrifying was about to unfold…

It was a normal day in Scotland. Raining as we went to school. And as we sat in the classroom, the power cut off. 'Creepy,' I thought. All the Primary Ones were crying, but we got on with it and did maths. All of a sudden, lightning struck a tree and we were told to evacuate. Then something happened that I never thought in a lifetime would happen…

All the clouds were moving and there was a hole in the middle of them. Then an enormous mountain appeared in the shape of a volcano. Lightning was striking everywhere. Out of the mountain came a dragon! As it emerged it destroyed everything in its path. It was terrifying. Then it attacked our school, ripping it half and breathing fire over it.

We all ran home to survive the danger, but our school was destroyed.

# St Augustine's
## by Sophie Anderson

St Augustine's is our school,
This school is the best.

Anyone can join our school,
Uniting our hopes and feelings,
Grow together and help one another,
Use your thoughts and feelings to spread it to others,
St Augustine's is amazing,
Teachers in our school are kind and helpful,
In our school everyone is kind,
Never be down; remember we are always here,
Everyone in this school is welcoming,
St Augustine's is the best school you will ever find.

# The Two Swans
## by Marianna Parker

In our street there is a pond. In the pond live many insects, birds and sometimes plants. But there are two birds that stand out to me. They are beautiful swans.

They usually come around at Christmas and leave in the early spring or later. It is as if the pond is their holiday home or stop off point. The swans are usually accompanied by two ducks and sometimes a heron.

The swans have lovely brilliant white feathers and vibrant orange beaks. Sometimes they like to sit on the water and sometimes they like to sit on the soft green grass.

This year, they haven't gone away just yet. But they sometimes fly away for day, weeks and maybe even a month. In the morning I love to see the swans together on the water. When the water is still and calm, and the sun is shining on the water, they like to wake up. My favourite time to see them is just when they wake up and stretch out their giant wings. They flap them hard, creating a splash and a gust of wind. Although swans can be dangerous, I will always think of them as fascinating, beautiful and elegant.

I love having the two swans in our street. I named them Rose and Giovani after the Strictly Come Dancing winners. I feel like it gives me something to look forward to seeing as I pass by. They bring a wee bit of sparkle to the pond. I hope that other people also like the swans as much as I do. And I hope they always come back.

# The Forever Tree
## by Darci Ellen O'Donohue

In the depths of the Great Woods stands the Forever Tree. It is huge. The bark on its trunk is smooth and grooved almost like the branches are bolted together.

There is something quite different about this tall tree; something strange, as if there is life inside.

One dark night, a woodcutter named Joe set off into the deepest part of the woods. He was hunting for some wild boar to feed his children.

Joe lived with his family in a small, quaint cottage buried deep in the roots of the forest.

He faced many dangers trying to provide for them. After many tiresome hours of searching, Joe finally fired his arrow over the misty, murky waters and killed his boar.

Suddenly, out of nowhere, this Forever Tree transformed into a monstrous tree-like creature. This terrifying figure then reached out and snatched Joe's wild boar.

Poor Joe stood very still and silent, camouflaged within the green forest. His legs were quivering with fear, but he would not give up his hunt...

Grace Hyland

# The Lighthouse
## by Orlaith Higgins

It begins many, many moons ago, in the year 1596, when the first flushing toilet was invented. In an old village, on an old island, stood a lighthouse. This lighthouse in particular was probably older than the Queen and 8.9 inches shorter than Big Ben. In the lighthouse lived an old lady and her dog called Kat. They lived a lovely life. But it all changed one dreadful, rainy night.

It was 7:49 am, when I would still be sleeping, but the old lady and the dog called Kat were eating breakfast when, 17 milliseconds later, there was a thud. That thud became a crash and later, a bang. They hurried up to the top of the lighthouse to find glass… Glass everywhere. And they quickly found where it came from. The bulb had broken and Kat, who was not a cat, went wild, running up and down.

Later that day, evening in fact, the old lady tried to fix the bulb. But a cruise ship was coming, and oddly fast. The lady started speeding through her tools, going as fast as she could. But she wasn't quick enough. She could see the ship…

And it stopped… The ship had stopped!

Turns out the captain knew what had happened and could see the island. He probably ate his carrots.

The old lady and Kat, who was not a cat, could go back to their normal lives and let someone else fix the bulb.

# Laughter
## by Maya Fergusson

Laughter is like a blanket the wraps you up in joy,
Laughter gives us hope in the darkest of dark times,
Laughter is like a disease;
It will spread and spread and spread,
But not a terrible, bad one; a good one instead.

We all hold laughter in our best moments,
Because it makes us happy and warm,
Laughter is the cure to sadness,
It always makes me smile.

Laughter is the medicine to life,
I recommend at least as dose a day,
Because laughter takes
All the misery away.

# The Abandoned Stadium
## by Christopher Wildman

It was Wednesday night, 7:43 pm, the 3$^{rd}$ of June 2062. I was walking down the street, getting a chippy. As I walked down Creel Drive I heard something. I realised as I was walking down the street it was getting louder and louder and louder until it was ear-splitting. Putting my headphones on, I turned and walked the other way.

This was a street I had never been down before. As my mum would say, it was, 'sketchy.' It was getting painfully loud. By the time I got to the end of the street the sound was raucous. But what I saw was indescribable.

Ever since I retired from professional football I'd not seen a stadium. But this was different. As I stood on the first concrete slab, all the noise stopped. Outside this zone sort of thing, it was loud. There were big green, blue and red flashing lights, with many food stalls outside. Though inside was dull, I could see the dust floating uncontrollably through the damp air. There were dead trees all over.

It was the Savannah Stadium. It was fully made of wood. It looked like it could collapse at any moment. I thought this was nothing to bother about. But then I heard a soul-destroying scream which could shatter ears. I decided to investigate.

As I walked on, I realised the floor was made of wood too, as it was constantly creaking. I was careful in case I broke anything. I got on the pitch and saw a young boy on a chair with fireworks attached. I released him and we ran out of the stadium just in time.

# Should Zoos Be Closed?
## by Charlotte Jackson

Zoos started appearing in 1793 and have been popular ever since. Zookeepers started treating their animals poorly and as a result people have lost their lives.

On one hand, animals are being fed and taken care of, whilst making people happy. Zoos protect animals from being poached and saving them from extinction. If we were to remove zoos, many animals would become extinct. Zoos also raise awareness of environmental problems.

On the other hand, animals have very limited space and it's very unnatural. Though zoos have an amiable exterior, it's no secret that most zoos do not take care of their animals properly. One of the biggest problems with zoos is the aforementioned lack of space, which leads to animals having bad mental health and losing sanity. That situation starts the Butterfly Effect of people losing their lives. Apathy costs people their lives.

After examining the evidence above, I strongly recommend that zoos should stay open, but bring back the passion people used to have for animals. Going to the zoo is a heavenly experience and I don't think we should take that away from people. We are blessed to have these incredible animals on our planet and we should not be trying to profit from them whilst we are making them unhappy.

# Sky Mountain
## by Gilbert Hagerty

The mountain is tall enough to reach Heaven. The clean air flies into my nostrils as I feel the velvety wet grass. It is lonely yet calm. Below me is the crystal clear loch, bluer than the blue skies. The top of the hill is so high it gives me the view of a hundred eagles. There are rocks at the top, some as sharp as knife; others velvety like a blanket. The trees, although oak, are as soft as a pillow after years of rain. Yet the leaves are quite hard and crunchy, like a crackling fire. Although looking grim, they feel quite luxurious.

# A Mission to Save the World
## by Mikee McKay

When I was born I had super powers. I had massive ears and a good sense of smell. So before I tell you about Kieran and George, my name is Mikee Mouse. Now Kieran. He was born with big ears like me. His family are very nice and he has fabulous hearing. Now George. He was born with no super power but he is very rich. He can be a nuisance. His favourite thing is to bribe you. We met at a café called the Mint.

We work for Super Scottish Men. It is run by Scottish people. They are nice and we were their first recruits. They told us we would work together and if we ever fail a mission we will be fired.

So we met up at the Mint and spoke about our job. After that we went to the park then **BANG!**

We rushed over and it was the biggest and richest bank in the world. We checked everywhere and found him in the Vault. Big Bojo. He steals but, worst of all, he breaks his own rules. He also parties all night. He threw something at us and it sent us back in time…

I was on top of the Eiffel Tower and I nearly fell off. I was very short of memory, but Kieran and George found me. We went to the bottom of the tower and there found Big Bojo kidnapping two women called called Maci-Jai and Darci. He forced them to work for him. George went after Maci-Jai and she won! She stole all of his money. Kieran went against Darci. I went against Big Bojo.

After defeating Darci, Kieran quickly saved George. I fought Big Bojo while they fought Maci-Jai. They found her on a building and got George's money back. So now it was the three of us against Big Bojo. He threw an orange and it exploded, incapacitating Kieran and George…

It was down to me.

I punched Big Bojo with a right hook and I won. I called the police and they locked him up.

George bought us a boat and we went the wrong way. We ended up in Portugal. After seven hours we got back. I was so happy because we were made leaders of Super Scottish Men. It was the hardest mission ever.

# Behind the Door
## by Eden Maria Mullen

I woke up to the sound of my door rattling. I was scared. I saw a bright light behind my door. I opened it and gasped. There was nothing there. I sighed as I said, 'I wonder…' My door was rattling again but louder now. I opened it again. 'There's a whole new world behind here,' I said to myself. I was so amazed I couldn't believe my eyes. It felt calm there, but I was too scared to go in. I quickly shut the door and went back to bed.

I could not stop dreaming about that place. It felt as if it were calling to me. But for what reason? I'd had enough! I marched up to my door and opened it. But there was nothing there. I realised it needed to be morning for it to happen again. I went back to bed so excited.

I woke up exhausted. I could smell bacon from the kitchen. I got dressed in my blue, ruffled tank top with my woolly cardigan that I knitted myself. Next I put on my baggy jeans and colourful Jordans. I chose those shoes and not my Converse because I was feeling very bright. I decided I wanted to have breakfast first. But before I could brush my hair, I heard, 'Sky! Time for breakfast!'

I replied, 'Coming Mum,' in a sweet tone. I brushed my brown hair as I glared at my hazel eyes in the mirror. My mum was happy I was going outside more and getting a tan. I'm already naturally tanned but my mum loves the Sun! My hair is naturally wavy and shiny. I'm about medium height and I love skateboarding. Also, I'm eighteen.

I touched my cold old door knob and the door creaked as I opened it. I raced down my old grey carpet to the stairs and asked my mum, 'Can I have some bacon up in my room?'

She replied, 'Yes Sweetheart.'

I grabbed my bacon and headed back upstairs. I ate as fast as lightning. I remembered what I had said: 'I wonder.' The door started rattling. I opened it and headed inside.

It was so magical with its waterfalls and rainbows. But then I felt my eyes growing blue. Suddenly I saw a mythical lion with a mane full of patterns and colours. Then he spoke to me and I understood him. He said, 'Welcome to Enchantra.'

'Wow!' I answered. 'This is amazing.'

'Yes,' said the lion. 'Until *this* happened. Follow me.' I followed him into a dark wood I never thought was there. Next thing I knew, everything was covered in stone and black dust. In the middle was a glowing staff trapped inside a black rock. It was shining an icy blue. Carved in the rock were two great hands.

'Pull the staff from the rock and all the stone and black dust will disappear. Our world will be renewed.'

I gazed at it. 'I can't pull that out.'

'Yes you can,' replied the lion. 'It's why you're here.'

I slowly walked towards the rock. There were little animals following me. 'Hello.'

'Hello,' said one. 'I am King, a little demon. You need to travel to get all the gems before you can take the staff from the rock. You need to travel to different worlds. Here, take this blue hoverboard. It will take you to the worlds.'

'Okay.'

'We will come with you,' said King.

'Me too,' added the lion. As I picked up the hoverboard he said, 'No, that's slower. Hop on my back.'

'Okay,' I said. 'Let's go.'

We headed to the first world, the Earth Realm. It was full of rocks and flowers. It was so wonderful. The lion said, 'Use your power.'

'What do you mean?'

'Your eyes started to glow when you came here,' he explained. 'It was your power. Go on, make us a tower that no one can get up to, where we can rest.'

'I'll try,' I said. I focussed all my power. It started to grow from underground. Everything was trembling. My eyes were glowing. I finally finished. I felt weak.

'Good job,' the lion congratulated me.

'Well done,' agreed King. We quietly rested while we thought where to look.

Then I had it! The Stone castle! We woke up and secretly headed to the palace, as quietly as mice. We got to the castle and climbed on the mossy green roof. There, through the window, we saw the green Earth Gem. With my powers I made a rope and climbed down. I swiftly grabbed the gem while no one was looking. Then I climbed back up. But it turns out someone did see me. I was caught! I ran and jumped on my hoverboard. I yelled, 'Come on guys,' and we all ran to the portal to the next realm.

The Air Realm was full of wind. There were cool vehicles made of wind. They all had something like a kite on their backs. We were looking around and saw a big airship in the sky. 'Jump on quick,' advised the lion. He had majestic wings that had all different colours on the feathers. We flew up into the clouds. I felt one. It was so soft I nearly fell asleep. We went up and up until we reached the airship. It was big and white with steam blowing quickly out of it. It was just floating out in the sky. I thought it was beautiful, but we needed that Air Gem. We hopped on the roof and slide quietly to the door to get in.

We snuck in quietly and King whispered, 'Wow, look how cool this is.'

'I know, right?' I replied. 'But we need to focus on the gems.'

'We need to put them in the stone hands so we can stop the stone dust,' explained the lion. 'Legends say the Chosen One breaks the spell.'

I froze. Then I just got on with my mission. We snuck into the main room. There was an old man there. We tried to run, but he locked the doors.

'Come now,' he said. 'We won't hurt you if it's the gem you seek.'

'Wow,' replied King. 'They're letting us take it.'

'No,' continued the old man. 'You must solve the puzzle.'

The lion said, 'Okay, tell us your riddle.'

The old man smiled. 'If it's the gem you seek, look at the sky. Go on, take a peek.'

We headed out the airship and up into the sky. 'Do you see it?' I gasped. 'Over there. In that cloud.'

We landed on a soft cloud and searched.

'There it is!' shouted King.

'Good,' said the lion. 'Let's go now. Quick!' We all hopped on his back and flew back to Enchantra. We went back through the portal and stood in front of the staff.

'Go on, put the gems in,' said King.

'Oh no!' I groaned. 'There's one space left. We're missing one.'

'Make it with you power,' suggested the Lion.

'No,' sighed King. 'That's impossible.'

But behind a tree I saw a strange wooden trap door. I walked towards it. 'What's this?' I asked myself. I opened the door. It made a screech. I swiftly jumped in. I felt nervous. I saw a stone and carved in it I saw a heart. And underneath, carved in the mossy stone it said, 'Do you think you are capable of the Love Gem? All place hands here and see if you are worthy.'

I gasped. This was the final gem. I called everyone over. 'Guys, come here! We need to put our hands here.'

'What for?'

'Look,' said King. 'It says the Love Gem.'

We all put our hands on the heart. It started glowing pink. The stone disappeared and out dropped a gem. We took the gem and placed it in the stone hands and the staff started glowing brighter. I quickly walked up to the staff and lifted it up. It started glowing brighter and brighter. The dust started disappearing and as it did, my bedroom was appearing. And as the last of the dust was gone, I was back home. Yawning, I headed back to bed, dreaming of my next adventure.

# Primary 7

Grace Haggerty

# The Lost Hat and a Surprise
## by Lucy Fern

Millie started the day with a big yawn, her hair half and half, purple and black. Millie slowly walked to her desk to wake up her pet snake Jaws. Jaws got really grumpy in the morning but Millie always woke him up to take him out his cage and stretch a bit more.

From the other side of the wall, she heard a lot of racket. It was her brother Joseph. Millie and Joseph had the same style of clothing; dark type of colours. Joseph's hair was mostly black with a tiny bit of dark blue.

Millie got ready to go to school in her favourite clothes. She liked to wear a dark blue and a light blue. But her most favourite thing that she never took off was her special green hat. Millie loved her lime green hat. She called it her lucky hat.

Every night she went to bed at midnight for three reasons. Millie loved the dark time. She got to make rock music all night when no-one else was up. And she had the full house to herself.

Sometimes Jaws got really angry because Millie might make a lot of noise. Joseph's pet hamster Sharp liked to go on his hamster wheel at night, which made Jaws get all grumpy in the morning because he didn't get enough sleep. And because Millie got him up really early too. He was so lazy that he would sleep all day.

When they came home from school, Millie checked on Jaws and Joseph checked on Sharp. Most of the time Jaws tried to get out of his cage and eat Sharp because Sharp was so loud when Jaws was trying to sleep.

Millie was wearing her hat and she went to the park with Joseph. There was a strong wind. Millie was almost getting blown over. She was sitting on the bench when the wind blew really hard. Her favourite lucky hat blew straight off her head. She and Joseph started chasing it everywhere… until it blew in the pond. She was very upset about it because she had that hat since she was five years old. Millie felt like it gave her strength and courage and personality.

Joseph said he would get her another one, but Millie was very, very upset and ran home to her room. She heard some weird voice and she said to herself, 'Yeah Joseph, stop putting on that voice to try to make me feel better.'

But she kept hearing it. It kind of sounded like the weird voice was saying, 'That stupid rat hamster mouse thing.'

Millie realised that the only person or thing it could be was Jaws. Millie jumped out of her bed and went over to Jaws' cage. She was shocked to see that it was Jaws. Jaws asked her where was her hat. But then he realised she didn't have her hat on.

# The Birthday Present That Changed the Future!
## by Shay McGonigle

One day in the poor Rio de Janeiro suburb of Bento Ribeiro, there was a boy named Cristiano who grew up loving football. He had always wanted a football to play with. But his family had just moved town and bought a house there, so they had no money. Cristiano was that desperate to play football that he rolled a pair of his socks up and began to kick them about. Cristiano was only four years old and already knew he wanted to be a footballer. For Cristiano's fifth birthday, his Mum Olivia and Dad Callum saved up to get him a football and cheap pair of football boots.

Cristiano went to sleep the night before his birthday thinking he wasn't getting anything. He woke up and walked downstairs very upset. But as he walked into the living room, he saw a bright shiny ball and lime green football boots. He rushed in, put them on and went straight outside. Cristiano then made some friends because he had a football. He spent all day playing with his new friends and new football. He was the best player out of the full friend group.

Cristiano was then noticed by a football school.

When Cristiano was thirteen he was attending high school. He continued his football school and was then signed for Partick Thistle Under 15s Football Academy. Cristiano was getting paid £20 for every training session he attended. And because he loved football, he attended every session. This meant in five days he was getting £100. Cristiano was now helping his family and they were very grateful. He was now addicted to playing football and started not going to school. Cristiano's Mum was okay with this and was proud of him for earning them money.

Cristiano had been training hard for weeks for his big game coming up, and he put loads of effort in. Saturday morning came. His game was at 9.30 am and he woke up at 6 am to go out a run. He went a two hour run and came back home to get ready. The time came and Cristiano's Mum left the house with him. His Dad was at work and was coming to watch the second half. Cristiano played in CM or right wing and he started on right wing. It was Partick Thistle vs Glasgow Red Star.

Right from kick off Partick Thistle scored the first goal. Later on that game Cristiano was playing amazingly because his Mum and Dad had told him there were scouts there. Cristiano wanted into a bigger and better team. So the game finished and Cristiano kept seeing the same guy watching him play.

After the game the scout came over to his Mum and Dad and said, 'I am a Scout from Celtic FC and we would like to take Cristiano and give him a trial.' Cristiano's Mum and Dad were very pleased and took him to the movies for a little treat. The date for his trial was the 20th of November 1901 and it was the 17th of November. So he had three days left and he could not wait.

The day came and he was a little big nervous. But it all went okay and he got signed. His first game for Celtic was a Celtic vs Rangers league decide game.

So that game came and Cristiano played from start to finish. He was amazing and the fans were cheering his name. He couldn't believe the atmosphere. But the clock ticked to the eighty-ninth minute and Cristiano broke through with the ball. The score was 1-1. Cristiano's eyes lit up and the next thing the fans erupted and burst into song cheering him. He had stopped Rangers from taking the league and that is where Cristiano made his name.

# Billy's Adventure
## by Rosa Cummings

Once upon a time a little boy called Billy was dreaming. He was dreaming about pirates. Billy was on an island with a population of one. But legend had it there was a majestical creature living in the waters surrounding the island.

Then, out of nowhere, Captain Ollie showed up. He was tall but plump and had only one eye. Captain Ollie demanded that Billy came with him to try and capture the majestical creature. Billy did as he said.

Just as the island was out of sight… **THUNDER!** Billy passed out! As he awoke he saw that Captain Ollie had fallen overboard during the storm!

Billy clung on to the rail as the ship tipped further and further to the side. It was the worst storm he had ever seen. With one powerful wave he felt himself being thrown across the deck. Terrified, he looked up and saw a flash of lightning illuminate the ocean. He gasped.

Just ahead of the ship he saw something splash in the ocean. He thought it was just the storm. But then he saw a tail. It must have been the majestical creature!

It used its powers to stop the storm…

When they got back to the island, they became best friends for ever. They lived happily ever after tormenting the monkeys.

# Fun/Boring
## by Komal Akhtar

Lockdown is fun,
But when family and friends can't come
It is very lonely.
You will miss them but love
Your sister, brother, mum and dad.

Lockdown is boring,
Only boring things to do all day,
Cooking can be fun,
But can be boring,
And can take your time up.

We've been in Lockdown quite a while,
It's getting hard to raise a smile.

# A Winter Bear
## by Filip Myslicka

The winter is a polar bear,
It's big and white,
It sleeps in cold places.
And bites the frozen grass.

The winter breathes on mountains,
And turns them into big snowballs,
It's dangerous when it's angry,
And can frostbite you.

In months after February,
It will hibernate for a while,
It will rise again in the dark months,
Perhaps November or December in the wild.

# The Four Disasters
## by Grace Haggerty

Covid is a blunder,
Covid is the thunder,
Covid should go away,
Even just for one short day.

Climate change is cold,
Climate change is bold,
Climate change is bad,
It makes us feel so sad.

Net zero is greenhouse gases,
Net zero is madness,
We should try to stop net zero,
We can all be a hero.

Russia and Ukraine are at war,
You can hear the bombs roar,
We all stand with Ukraine,
They are forced to play the game.

# The House
## by Aarran Innes

I live in a regular town, in a regular house, with regular friends but the one thing that isn't regular is the house across the street from me. The doors and windows are always open even though no one currently lives there. It's a dark grey colour with cracks all over the walls. The roof is a brown colour with a humongous hole in the middle and every time you walk past it you always have this weird feeling to stay away from it! One time when I walked past it, it felt like someone, or something was watching me. That night I had a nightmare where the house grew legs and arms and then tried to eat me. After that night I decided that I was going to find out what was going on inside that house and why people always get weird feelings when they walk past it.

I have been planning on sneaking into that house for a while now, but tonight is perfect as my parents are going out for dinner. So, if I just quietly sneak past my older sister's bedroom, she won't even know that

I'm gone. The next part of the plan is simple: go into house and explore.

'Isabella!'

'Yes mum?'

'We're leaving now don't cause any trouble and be good to your sister.'

'Ok Mum bye!'

'Bye; love you!'

And just like that they're gone. Now I just need to figure out a way to sneak out of the house. My older sister has the key to front door and back door. I know what to do! I'll tie my sheets and blankets together to make a rope to climb down my bedroom window. I throw my sheets and blankets out the window to climb down. My bedroom is on the second floor so if I fall it will be a big fall. But against all odds, I manage to climb down the rope safely and there it is.

As soon as I look up at the house, I feel that feeling again.

'No!' I say out loud. 'I'm not scared anymore.' I sprint into the house not looking back and run inside. Once I inside, I look around. There is a small kitchen in front of me. The living room on my left. Wooden stairs leading up. I enter the kitchen first. It smells like rotten fish. It is extremely dirty. The walls have green and brown stains all over them. There are also cracks all over the roof and even some on the walls too. The next room I go into is the living room. There is a TV on the floor, smashed with broken glass all over and around it. There is a sofa too. It is red, but it looks like a wild animal ripped it apart. The ceilings and walls also have cracks all over them. 'Why are there so many cracks everywhere?' I think to myself. Next is upstairs. I begin to walk up the stairs. Every time I take a step up it makes this horrible and loud screeching sound. While I am walking up the stairs, I notice a painting of a little boy. He is wearing what looks like a school uniform. Then all of a sudden, a massive crack appears in front of me. It starts spreading and getting bigger. I run up the stairs like lighting. After a few minutes they stop.

I look up. It is just a door. No other rooms upstairs. Just one door. I try to open it, but it won't budge. I step back and run up to the door and kick it down. I fall into the room and look up. There is a chest in the middle of the room. I pick it up and open. It is just an old necklace. It is golden and has a diamond attached to it. Suddenly the cracks start appearing all over the room. Then a chunk of the roof started falling on me. I sprint out of the room as fast I as I can. A massive chunk of the roof falls on the stairs causing them to collapse. I scream as the stairs start to crumble to the ground. I push all the rubble off me. I sprint towards the exit and manage to barely get of there alive. I run over to the rope that I made and begin climbing up. Then I jump into my room. I let out a sigh of relief; finally home. That day the entire house collapses. Even though I almost died I manged to grab that necklace. When I look at the necklace, I can remember this day.

# Peace for the Planet
## by Sam Broadley

The cities are burning,
My life is turning upside down,
Russia are invading,
My life is fading.

All I want is peace,
Peace for the planet!

The sirens are moaning,
While the city is going,
The planes are coming,
Everybody running.

All I want is peace,
Peace for the planet!

In the distance you hear screams,
At night you see beams of light,
Guns are shooting,
Buildings are fuming.

All I want is peace,
Peace for the planet!

My dad is away fighting,
My mum is crying,
Little kids not understanding,
Families dying.

And all I want is peace,
Peace for the planet!

# The Lockdown Lovings
## by Kal McHenry

Even though Lockdown was a pain,
We still did some things that did gain,
More time with friends and gaming all day,
There are still things that we did,
To train for the school quiz behind the computers.

The meaningful time with family all day,
And kick-up football challenge with toilet paper,
People crying out, 'Hooray!'
When they NHS save the day.

Facetime with a family groupchat,
Or texting friends on snapchat,
It all gains a relationship with friends and family.

Even though we're crying thick tears,
And least we're not pulling out our hair,
Because we're in a safe environment called home.

# The Paper Plate Cat Burglar
## by Kai Williams

It was a dark night during the month of April. All you could hear was the sound of cars passing by, including a black van racing down the road with four police cars following behind with blaring sirens that could be heard a mile away. Money flew out the van like water in a fountain as the plain black van drifted around corners until it disappeared. The police sirens turned off, filling the street with silence. The things left were trails of stolen money and a paper plate mask with a poorly drawn cat face on it. Nobody saw where they went.

Later, a man with a dark grey hoodie obscuring his face lay a duffle bag on a table in the middle of his house. The house had peeling grey wallpaper, flickering lights and an old, moist carpet. The man went into his kitchen and grabbed a paper plate. He drew a face on it before hiding it in a cabinet. The next day he woke up to banging at the door, followed by shouting. The door burst open and police found no one home, just a wide open window.

When the police left, the man went into his garage and pressed a button on the old, dusty wall. The button turned a bookshelf into a gun rack holding rifles, grenades and lots of paper plates.

Later that night, the man approached a museum. Using a crowbar he prised open the door. But as soon as they opened the alarms went off. Within minutes police officers swarmed into the building and arrested the burglar and gave him life in prison.

**'THE PAPER PLATE CAT BURGLAR IS FINALLY CAUGHT!'** was all over the news. On top of being captured and imprisoned, the entire world knew everything about him: his name, his age, what he looked like; everything.

The prison guards threw him into a cell with dark, mossy brick walls and a bed that felt like stone. An old TV sat in the corner playing the news broadcast about his capture. Minutes felt like days as he sat in the cell with no one around.

Suddenly two officers opened the door and ordered him to go to the cafeteria for lunch. There, people were screaming and fighting like wild animals. He saw this as an opportunity to escape. While a guard was breaking up a fight, he stole the keys and ran outside to the front of the prison. The guards followed but one of the police cars was racing away with him at the wheel.

The Paper Plate Cat Burglar had escaped…

# The Beast of the East
## by Michael O'Neill

The ocean is a beast
With big yellow teeth,
He's fierce and tall,
He roars and crawls,
He will swallow you in
With a frightening grin,
He lives in the East,
Dying for a feast.

He sleeps on the sand,
Staring at the land,
Desperate to eat,
He can smell human meat,
He's oh so old,
And oh so bold,
He will snap and bite
When he comes out at night.

# Life During Lockdown
## by Josh Molloy

What a laugh,
While looking at the clock ticking,
Sitting down by the fire,
Or seeing people pump up a tyre.
Life goes by while having fun,
Like playing FIFA,
Or going for a run.

Every Thursday we clap for the NHS,
Mass on Sunday on live TV,
We always got a Just Eat,
And the food was scoops and treats,
Waffles, ice cream, sweets galore,
Playing FIFA, going mental playing Maestro.
Life in Lockdown was fun.

# Cosy Cottage
## by Emily O'Donnell

Once upon a time, in a village called Lecunshire, there lived a girl called Orlaith Sharrat. She was quite tall. She had auburn hair with light curls. She had freckles on her face and bluey green eyes with really long eye lashes. She loved to read and she loved cats. She was twenty-one, Irish and loved to bake. She had her own bakery called the Tiddles Bakery, named after her beautiful tortoiseshell cat. She had two pet snails also; one called Lettuce and one called Leaf. They were lovely and very friendly too.

She loved making very tasty scones. The recipe had 5 kg of raisins, 3 kg of flour, 3 tablespoons of vanilla extract, 1 kg of vegetable oil, 7 kg of sugar, and 4 kg of milk. That made 750 scones. She sold them at the bakery and they were the most popular goods. But sourdough bread was very popular too.

She lived in a cosy countryside cottage and loved to go for walks. Sometimes Tiddles went too. They would go down to the pond. Sometimes Tiddles tried to fish for tadpoles, but Orlaith told her, 'No Tiddles. Those tadpoles aren't food because they turn into baby frogs. And the frogs would grow in your tummy. And we don't want that, do we?'

Sometimes Orlaith and Tiddles had picnics in the countryside. Orlaith brought food from the bakery. She would give Tiddles fish that Mr and Mrs Windsor had handed in for the cat. It was lovely smoked salmon. Tiddles loved it though Orlaith wasn't keen; she preferred cookies or scones or a nice Victoria Sponge cake. After the picnic they would go back to the cottage and feed the snails.

# Troubled World
## by Lennon McDade

Bang! Bang! Bang! The shots go off,
Ukraine is scared,
Putin is not,
The rest of the world sit back and pray.

Sea levels are rising; there's loss of habitat,
Trees are still falling after all that,
Polar bears' home is melting,
Trees keep falling, not helping.

Covid is deadly, people are dying,
Lots of us are still crying,
Coughing a lot, scared for me,
Oh no, it's Covid; it cannot be.

Our world is troubled,
Our problems have doubled,
It's very hard, I know it is,
Times have been worse, it will eventually fix.


# Lockdown
## by Harvey Blair

We've been in Lockdown for quite a while,
It's getting hard to raise a smile.
Sometimes have to force a grin,
But everything is wearily thin.

They crowd the beaches,
Pack the parks,
And queue for hours outside of Marks.

Will Boris even find a way,
Or lead us back to yesterday?
So on we go without a ruler,
Will we stay or will we slay?
Tomorrow's bright but for now please,
Stay home and pray.

# Storm Wolf
## by Ryan Peden

A storm is like a wolf,
Dark, scary and fluffy,
He runs and howls all night long,
He gnaws at the clouds.

The white fur is like lightning,
The clouds are grey and fluffy,
The wind howls like a wolf,
He prowls around the sky.

Stalking round and round,
The rain his razor-sharp teeth,
Coming upon you,
No way to stop it.

# The Amazing Team
## by Joshua Macinnes

William Steelman was just an ordinary guy who lived in an ordinary apartment in America. It had everything someone would need. Well, someone who doesn't need much. He got excited over nothing really. He lived down the street from a rich businessman named Juno. Juno wore a top hat, suit and had a cane. He had a weird accent that was definitely noticeable. And he wore colourblind glasses. Or so he said. William thought they were something else. William himself wore a red t-shirt and black trousers. He had blue eyes and, most notably, brown hair.

One day when William was watching TV the news came on. 'We have to interrupt this episode of Emmertale Barn,' announced John Evergreen, news reporter. 'We have been told that a strange figure has been roaming around near where a businessman's company is. We have live footage of a press conference. We'll go to that now.'

The picture switched to the press conference where Juno was saying, 'We will have zee thing sorted out soon enough. After all, we wouldn't want it here, would we?'

'Wow. That's not good,' thought William.

'Also, there has been strange lightning that keeps striking a mountain. And inside the same mountain there have been found structures,' continued John Evergreen, news reporter.

'Hmm… I wonder where that is?' After checking the map, William went to find the mountain. It was somewhere in the South. When William arrived he walked up to the mountain and touched it. It was as if it was hypnotic; as if it was mesmerising. Out of nowhere lightning struck William. It instantly knocked him out.

When he started to wake up he was weak and hurt. He heard singing or mumbling. Usually the two don't sound the same but they did this time. The voice sounded like a robot human… a cyborg!

'You're a lucky man, Mr Steelman,' said… who?

'Who… who are you?'

A figure approached him. It looked like he had four robotic arms that he was walking on. One of his eyes was brown; the other was glowing red. He looked like a cyborg, as William had thought. 'My name is Jake.'

'J… Jake?,' said William.

'Yes,' replied Jake.

'How am I lucky?' asked William.

'You are alive. Severe burns, broken bones… Yet you're somehow alive.'

'Well that's good,' said William.

'I can fix you.'

When William heard this his face had a scared look on it. 'How so?'

'With a needle. I found some… things that could save you.'

'Why didn't you save yourself?' asked William.

'I wanted this,' explained Jake, sounding angry. He injected William with the needle, saving him. 'I'll take the bandages off now.'


Millionaire, inventor, secretive… Juno was a lot of things. There have been theories he's been killed before; one half of his DNA was his, the other half a monster. The Chief of police tried to arrest him… he went missing years ago. Most of the evidence the police have was secret. Juno had been said to be a bad man for ages, but there had never been much proof.

'Ugh! I hate zees fools!' groaned Juno. 'How is zee operation, Mr Frond?'

'It is going well, Sir,' replied Mr Frond.

'Yes, yes, yes,' said Juno. 'But zee mountain?'

'Someone got struck by it, Sir,' admitted Mr Frond.

'Ha, ha, ha. Who?' While being rich he was also insane.

'He is okay now.'

'What? What? WHO?'

Mr Frond gulped. 'William Steelman, Si… Sir.'

'Send a team to bring him here!'

'Steelman!' shouted Jake.

'What is it?' asked William.

'Have you heard about Juno? He has machines to make humanity bow down to him.'

'How do you stop that?' wondered William.

'You either kill Juno or destroy the machine. I have intel.' There was a crack and a beep. 'Run!'

They ran out Jake's little house just before it blew up. Standing before them was a man holding a gun. 'I am Steve, a bounty hunter. I've been sent to get you.'

As Steve raised his gun, Jake lunged at him with his robotic arms. William ran around the small fight. He choked Steve from behind then kicked the gun off him. 'Who sent you?'

'Juno,' said Steve. 'Do you not like Juno?'

Jake and William both replied, 'No.'

'Neither do I,' said Steve. 'I hate his guts. I want to see him go down as much as you.'

'Well,' explained Jake, 'we are going to stop him.'

'Can I come?' asked Steve.

Jake and William discussed this. After deciding Steve could join them, William asked, 'How will we get there?'

Steve smiled. 'I have a helicopter. It came with the contract.'

So they flew right into Juno's base. Juno sent guards to kill them. Steve shot the guards and Jake punched them with his metal arms. Steve threw a grenade to William. 'Throw it at the machine, William!'

William threw the grenade and destroyed the machine, saving the world.

## Standing Strong
### by Leah McGuinness

In Lockdown I went on walks with my dog,
When we go on walks we find all types of logs,
Watching frogs jump about,
Laughing about blackouts.

All night long,
Waking up to the light,
And the sound of birds chirping,
Boiling pasta for my nan's dinner.

Whispering to friends all day long,
Every Thursday standing strong,
Getting stressed when watching the news,
Snoozing all day long.

Arguing about who's right or wrong,
listening to songs all day long,
and sleeping all day but still tired.

# A True Story (Or Is It?)
## by Grace Gaffney

One Friday afternoon Dexter was sitting at the door waiting for Grace to come in from school. As the door opened Dexter purred and leapt into Grace's arms. Grace took Dexter upstairs. Dexter examined the room and saw Grace's art desk, then spotted a pencil, pounced, and started chewing the end of it.

'DEXTER!' Grace shouted as she picked him up. 'Do not chew pencils!' She tapped him on the nose. Slowly she smiled and took the pencil out of the cat's mouth. Dexter wanted to go see Ripley but he was too lazy. At that moment Ripley walked in and meowed. Ripley was a happy, cheerful kitten who loved to spend time with Dexter. She tapped Dexter and he started to chase her…

How do I know so much about these cats, you may be asking? Well, I am Dexter and this is my story.

On October 31st 2021, I was picked up by a wonderful family called the Gaffneys. As soon as I saw Grace my eyes sparkled. I was so happy. She petted me and tickled my belly. I love her. She is always caring and kind. But let me tell you a story about her and a cat called Bilbo…

On the 27th of July work was getting done at Grace's house. They went to their Gran's and Grace's little cousin asked her to stay. Grace said yes. The next day she went home and Bilbo was missing.

They put up posters, even on websites like Missing Cats Scotland. But still to this day Bilbo is missing. That is why she never lets me out of her sight; she does not want it to happen again.

Grace loves me and I love her. I help her out with her art by taking her pens and it turns out she needs the colour but didn't know. But anyway, I want to introduce you to the family.

Firstly, the oldest cat of us all Gin, named after Qui-Gon Jinn from *Star Wars*; a handsome ginger cat. Catniss, after Katniss Everdeen from *The Hunger Games*; a stunning blue British Shorthair with dark amber eyes. Harley, after Harley Quinn from *DC*; a striped British Shorthair with light amber eyes. Kitty, named after what Boo called Sulley in *Monsters, Inc.*; a dark blue British Shorthair with dark amber eyes. Me, Dexter, named after the TV show *Dexter*; a lilac British Shorthair with amber green eyes. Ripley, my girlfriend, named after Ripley in *Alien*; a light blue British Shorthair with light amber eyes.

Well, that's my family and hopefully Bilbo will come back soon. He's a white British Shorthair with grey highlights and blue eyes. He's named after Bilbo Baggins from *The Hobbit* and *The Lord of the Rings*. I hope he comes back to join the family.

# Lockdown
## by Ciara Mullen

Lockdown was quiet,
But not in my house,
There were games nights,
With arguments all of the time,
Cheering all night when I won a game,
And going to bed at the latest of time.

In the morning of our mad night,
That day there was peace and quiet,
With no car engines roaring,
The only sound outside was the slightest of chirping,
And in the green forest some great games await.

On those school days when the Teams meetings start,
And we hunt for items,
We have no clue apart,
We will share our day and have a great laugh,
And when the teacher is teaching,
We will gain some great smart.

My favourite thing to do,
Is phone my friends, have a great laugh,
And cheer at the end.

For all those who don't know what Lockdown is,
It is fun,
It is boring,
It is all in between.

# Lockdown
## by Chloe Docherty

NHS are very important,
Especially when Covid-19 hit,
Hospitals – ambulances – cleaners – carers,
Are all supporting us,
To stop us being virus sharers,
Food shops, delivery men and women,
None of them are superhuman,
Let's do our part,
And have a heart.

# The Lost Tale
## by Kyle Robertson

Far in Iceland in a mountain range, it looked as though a meteor hit and made a hole, and in that hole lay a stunning village. All you could see were kids running about, happy people, smoke coming out all the small huts, and marvellous farmland. This glamourous village was called Mistic because of its mist and a myth. This myth was apparently told by every parent and grandparent. It was the tale of Enzo.

Enzo was the lovely but big dragon belonging to the princess Faith. She was a lovely girl but her father was terrible to her. The only thing her dad would give to her was Enzo. They had a very special bond. But one day Faith's father took Enzo from her for no reason. They were both in despair. Enzo waited and waited for days but Faith never came for him. So Enzo finally gave up. He opened his mouth and the sky turned orange with his heartbroken flames bursting into the night sky. He flew into the moon. All that could be seen was his drooped shadow. He landed in the cave of Axel. He changed, became angry and forgot what human life was like…

On the 12$^{th}$ of April 1865 the sun was slowly rising as the sky turned a bright orange. The moon was slowly fading away into the orange sky. Jackson woke up from his beauty sleep. He was a young man who only had a dad and a sister. But his dad was very ill and sister very young. He still loved his life very much. He had many friends and was a blacksmith, forging many cool swords and useful tools.

By now not many knew or believed in the tale of Enzo. Jackson knew but did not believe. There were only a few people left in the village who believed. The only reason they did was because of the crashes, bangs and loud noises they heard in the cave of Axel.

After he woke, Jackson got right to work after making sure his dad and sister were okay. Jackson noticed that he always forged with iron and wanted to use something else. But he could not, so he carried on working. Once he was finished he made sure everything was fine at home and then went out with his friends.

They decided to go to the cave of Axel. No one was allowed there but they still went. As they were walking down into the cave they saw a special orange glow. They went to investigate and found it was a big rock. They were quite fond of the rock and Jackson thought it would be great for forging with. As soon as he picked it up he saw it said on the bottom, 'To kill Enzo.' Then growls, rumbles and bangs started to happen. They sprinted out, scared to the point of shaking.

Jackson got right to work the next day and made a shiny set of armour and an orange glowing sword. He set off towards the cave to kill Enzo. He entered and walked a bit. He turned a corner and he saw a massive dragon staring him down, fire bursting through his nose. He had heard Jackson coming!

Jackson raised his sword and Enzo pounced!

It was an epic battle, Jackson getting hurt and Enzo getting hurt. But finally Enzo lurched at Jackson and Jackson's sword went through his mouth.

And the beast hit the floor.

## Memories of Lockdown
### by Liam Herlihy

Lockdown was good and bad,
But some of the memories that came from it
Are the best I've ever had.

Like when school was off,
We could spend more time with our family,
And play games like Scrabble,
While having a little battle.

When the sun shines,
We close our blinds,
And maybe play games,
Or go out in the garden
And chat up some dames.

It's good to watch movies and eat,
Even if the house is not neat,
Even if you're not even
Drinking out of a cup,
You shouldn't ever give up.

# The Maze of Doom!
## by Lauren Docherty

There was a ten year old girl called Sophie and she had a little dog called Lucky. Sadly Sophie was an only child and had no one to play with. But her mum had a plan and had organised a special treat: Sophie was going to the carnival. She was super excited and even Lucky was allowed to come.

When the day came, Sophie got up super early so she could get dressed up all fancy for the carnival. When it was time to go even Lucky was super excited. When they got to the carnival it was a little late, so all the big bright lights were shining and all the music was playing. The carnival was really loud but Sophie didn't care. She was too busy playing lots of games with Lucky and her mum.

An hour later a new game had just opened up and it was called *The Maze of Doom!* It was all lit up green and orange. Sophie and Lucky had decided to give it a go. But they would not do it without her mum. So they all went in. Inside it looked a little bit spooky, but Sophie and Lucky were very brave even though Mum was a little scared.

When they got halfway in the maze something went wrong. Sophie and Lucky became lost. They couldn't find Sophie's mum *ANYWHERE*. Sophie was very scared. She knew that she and Lucky had to get out of the maze. But as I said, they were halfway which meant they were lost. And even worse, they were alone.

One hour later Lucky and Sophie finally got out. Luckily they were safe. But they still couldn't find their mum. So they decided to go get help. They finally found a security guard. The guard looked for hours and hours, but still no mum. Sadly none of the security guards could find her.

An hour later Mum was finally found. Soon after, Sophie, Lucky and Mum went to McDonald's. Sophie had a burger, Mum had nuggets, and Lucky the dog got biscuits. The next day they had a relaxing time and Mum got a call saying *The Maze of Doom!* had shut down.

## Lockdown
### by Lucia Russo

As the days got warmer and the trees grew taller, Lockdown had just begun. People played boardgames and more. And there wasn't a day where people were bored.

There were lots of sunny days, lying on your back with your shades, while lunch was being made. Lots of birds in the sky, but no clouds while the grass was still dry.

Everyone had online learning, getting to see your friends until the meeting came to an ending. Outside playing with your sibling while you watched the hot tub dribbling.

Although it was hard being inside, we still tried to combine lots of fun stuff, while all the playing made Mum's mess tough, and playing in the mud made her washing rough.

Every Thursday we clapped for the NHS, clattering pots and pans. Facetiming family members, we remember memories before Covid together. Now Lockdown's over, we remember the sunny days and we remember the fun.

# Ninjas
## by Joe Potter

It all started in Japan, up in the foggy mountains where you could barely see the summits. One day a boy, who didn't have a name, went up one of the mountains. He saw what looked like an abandoned big house. Then he saw ninjas. They were in defence mode and so had to protect the Chief.

The young boy said, 'I want to be a ninja.'

The Chief came out and said, 'Okay. Stand down everyone. We could use another ninja.' So they let him in.

That night the young boy got his own room and he went to bed. The next morning they all got up and began training. A ninja mainly has a log first, so the young boy had to kick a log multiple times and punch it. So after a couple of years training he was ready to be a ninja.

He appeared on a building one night. There was a big puff of smoke. He had a black robe on with a pair of ninja stars and nunchucks. He also had a katana, a big silver katana. It was his pride and joy. He loved jumping around and helping people. He loved to help other ninjas. He also loved to train. Whenever there was a fight, he was always there first. They had trackers. If they flashed red it meant, 'Send other ninjas to help and assist.' If they flashed green it meant, 'It is okay and they are okay.'

One day he went out to look for danger. A gang of people were trying to get their friend out of a police van. Next thing you know, guns are blazing. The young ninja was in danger. The Chief saw this on the radar. He sent more ninjas down there. Then the Chief was in trouble! Helicopters, motorbikes and cars were seen going up the mountain. The Chief ran and sounded the alarm; it had never been used in years.

The ninjas rushed to the base. They had emergency ninja stars; they were explosive. The ninjas grabbed and threw them. Everything blew up in flames.

The bikes flew into the air. The cars flipped over. The choppers disappeared; they had retreated. The Chief was lucky. Now the ninjas had to return to the fight down in the city.

Two ninjas remained to protect the Chief. He went for a wee nap because of all he had just been through. The two ninjas went to where the cars and the bikes were. They could see organs. And blood gushing out of the cars. And arms, legs, hands, fingers and more. The cars were on fire. The two ninjas tidied it all up.

Down in the city the other ninjas sorted the gang problem. Then they headed back home.

# Tiger in the Sky
## by Thomas Parker

The wind is a vicious tiger,
Angry and strong,
Clashing with its prey,
Destroying everything in its way.

Crashing at high speeds,
Leaping and screaming a loud cry,
While swiftly passing by,
Swooping ferociously.

But when the time turns to night,
The previous roars are now very light,
It lies down quietly,
And sleeps without movement.

# Lost in Lavender City
## by Casey Allan

One stormy night in a cold dark science lab, there was a man called Professor Dork. He had a pet dog called Professor Bark. The man had rainbow spikey hair. He wore circled black glasses. He had one brown eye and one blue eye. He had no family, so he hated humans. For twenty years he had never left the lab. He couldn't remember what the real world looked like.

Professor Dork was experimenting on a new potion. He tested it by drinking it. In the blink of an eye he appeared in the middle of Lavender City. He and Professor Bark looked at one another with confused faces. There were lots of people with funky clothes, crazy hair, big dogs, small dogs and dogs in handbags.

All the shops were designer stores; Gucci, Louis Vuitton, YSL, Chanel and Move. There were lots of people in the streets selling things like toys, clothes, hats, shoes, footballs, soap, bath bombs, water bottles, books and lots more.

Professor Dork and Professor Bark walked around the streets for hours and hours trying to find somewhere to live. They had no luck until they turned a corner and saw a motel. They quickly ran over and booked a room for the night.

In the morning they got up and had breakfast. 'Ugh! I hate people,' said Professor Dork.

That same afternoon they left the motel and started walking. They came across an abandoned mansion. It was covered in leaves, mould, holes and trees. When they walked in Professor Dork felt a very cold breeze. Everything he said echoed through the whole house. Professor Bark went up the stairs and saw a picture of a man with purple hair and square glasses. Professor Dork joined him for a closer look. He read the name on the picture frame and it said, 'Professor Mork.' Their names did rhyme but he thought nothing of it.

Professor Dork's phone started to ring. It was from an unknown number. He heard a deep, crackly voice say, 'Hello Professor Dork. I am your father.'

The professor paused for a second. Then he asked his dad to meet him. When he arrived, his dad had purple spikey hair and was very tall.

They became very close and renovated the mansion. They still live there and are still making amazing potions.

## Killing Covid
## by Caoimbe Tuite

That time in 2020, parks were closed, shops were shut and schools were empty. We all stayed away to stay safe and healthy. We washed our hands just in case.

Often we laughed, but sometimes we cried, because it was different staying inside. The world has changed, let's hope for good. We had to stay safe; we all understood.

We missed our family, we missed out friends. Let's hope this isn't for long and we get back together; go out for dinner, parties and more.

# Hitman
## by Lewis Allison

It was a brisk Tuesday morning when Stephen was out in the forest. All he could hear was the ribbiting of frogs and the calls of birds. He could smell the freshness of the brisk wind hitting his face. Everywhere he looked there were palm leaves bigger than humans and trees bigger than a building.

Stephen was six feet three in height. He had blond hair, brown eyes and a little facial hair. Stephen was a professional hitman trained to kill high ranking drug dealers. In return he would get £2 million for each murder. Stephen was in the forest to kill the number one ranked drug dealer in the world. His name was Pablo. Pablo was the biggest dealer, wit ties to the Russian cartel. Stephen had him surrounded; the forest was filled with members of his team. Stephen surely had him! But then Pablo had an underground bunker and the Russian cartel came and picked him up.

Stephen was heartbroken. He went to his house, sat on his grey velvet couch and had a red whisky. He was devastated. He dozed off but when he was about to fall into a deep sleep, he got a call from an unknown number. He answered.

It was Pablo.

Pablo had his best friend hostage and said he would shoot him if Stephen didn't give him £100 million!

Stephen jumped off his couch and went down the crooked stairs towards the basement. He opened the door and grabbed an MK-Seven assault rifle and an auto shotgun. He stuffed two grenades in his pocket and made a few calls. His team came in choppers and motorbikes. Pablo had messed with the wrong people.

Stephen ran upstairs and slowly jumped out the back window to climb the hill. He saw Pablo. But while Stephen lined up a shot, Pablo was gone in a chopper and on his way to Bangladesh. Stephen and his crew took a plane to Bangladesh. Pablo would import illegal substances from South America. Stephen had the drop site covered in men. Pablo could not escape this time.

Stephen jumped from the roof and punched Pablo. Suddenly the Russian Cartel arrived. But so did Stephen's team. It was an all out brawl. But in the end Stephen and his team were the victors.

# Glasgoo
## by Orla Brady

It started off in the year 3202. Tobey Invis was at his job in Glasgow. Tobey was just sitting at his desk stamping books in the library. Later on after his shift was over, he was walking home past the carnival. A strange old man with a long coat walked by him and kept offering him an old bobble hat. Tobey then said, 'Well, it is cold and my head is freezing, so I will take your hat.'

When Tobey was home he started to have very bad thoughts about the hat the old man gave him. His curiosity got the better of him because he put the hat on and everything was different. All the essentials in his home were covered in a strange sticky neon goo. His fridge, his sink and his boots were all covered. When he went to his bathroom the door was covered in the same sort of goo, but it was much stronger than the original goo!

The next morning before work, Tobey passed by the carnival looking for the old man. But he was nowhere to be found. By the time Tobey had finished searching, he put on the bobble hat. When he got to the library, it was sort of similar to his home. All of the books were covered in that strange goo, but when he went to the bathroom, it was covered in that stronger goo.

While Tobey was exploring this very strange place, out of nowhere he heard a very deep gurgle. Tobey got so scared that he ran outside and thought,

'Whatever this nightmare is, I'm getting out of it.' And he ripped the hat off and left it in the office.

Tobey kept thinking about what he heard with the hat on. What he did next was crazy. He got a big sword and put the hat on. As he was shifting into this crazy world, he thought to himself, 'Whatever this is, I'm going to finish it.' Once he was in his home in the other dimension, he ran outside and yelled, 'Come on you beast!'

All of a sudden he heard loud thuds coming from the distance. A quick think from Tobey and then he started climbing up a building. When the monster got to him, without thinking twice Tobey jumped into mid air. With his sword he landed on the monster's back. Tobey stabbed the monster and it fell to the ground. A volcano of goo burst out.

As Tobey stared at the monster he said, 'I am a hero and no one will ever know.' As Tobey was slowly taking off the hat and returning to his own world, he started crying, thinking, 'My mother and father weren't here to see any of this.'

## The Storm
## by Emily McDines

The storm is an angry wolf,
He's giant and grey,
And hungry for prey,
He batters and howls,
Against the window he growls,
He's crazy and wild,
But stay inside and he's mild.

He huffs and he puffs
To make the wind come down,
He's loud and he's proud,
He makes it rain all day,
But nothing can make this wolf go away.

He thrashes and crashes
Against the woods until dawn,
But happy as ever, it's sunny,
All day long.

He's sun and he's fun,
Until someone makes him mad,
You'd better run 'cause he won't,
He snores and he roars,
From night until dawn,
Now he's happy everyone's gone.

## System Failure
### by Harry Spalding

One rainy morning Isabella woke up, got out of her wooden bed and walked over the newly fitted carpet to flick the light switch and wake up her siblings.

'I don't understand how the alarm doesn't wake you up!' she pointed out while grabbing her school uniform and phone from the dresser. 'Anyways Jose, Mum wants you.'

Isabella walked across the hall to the bathroom to get ready. She reluctantly took her toothbrush and toothpaste out of the medicine cabinet and brushed her very shiny white teeth. 'Bleh!' she stuttered while spitting the leftover toothpaste into the sink. She left the bathroom and went downstairs to see Mum. She went to the bottom of the hall to the kitchen. 'Hiya Mum,' she said while she sat down.

'Hello Isabella, your breakfast is on the table,' Mum told her.

'Thank you. I'm going to be late, so can you drive me to school just now?'

'Okay,' sighed Mum.

Isabella quickly put on her President badge and opened the car door. She was about to run when Mum stopped her, saying, 'Wait! Share this bag of snacks with your friends.'

'I told you I didn't want this!' exclaimed Isabella while taking it and running to the gate. The start of school was always the most stressful time of the day. Large crowds of students were waiting at traffic lights. The Headteacher would always wait at the gate with a timer. He would always make anyone who was late, even just by a second, put their name on a board. Isabella ran as fast as she could to get in as soon as possible. She got through the gate with one second to spare. She walked to the entrance of the school and over to her locker. She changed her shoes so that there would be no mud in the school. Once she finished she walked down the crowded hallway.

Isabella arrived at her First Period class and sat down to study. There was a group of boys talking. Samuel was sitting on somebody else's desk. Elizabeth walked in and saw him. 'Hey! Get off my desk!' she yelled.

'Woah! What happened to you?' asked Samuel. 'You're usually calm.'

Elizabeth took a book out her bag and hit his hand. 'I SAID GET OFF MY DESK!'

'Ow! Chill,' laughed Samuel while walking away.

Elizabeth sat down as if she was holding a huge grudge.

The teacher finally walked in. 'Alright you lot. Settle down. Hand your phones.' Everybody got up, row by row, and handed in their phones. Once everyone had handed them in she noticed something. 'Samuel? This is you phone from last year. Take it back and hand in your real phone. Oh, also, Isabella? The Student Council has been asked to take over detention, so you're free to leave.'

'Yes Ma'am,' replied Isabella while standing up to leave.


Isabella stepped out of her class and closed the door. She made her way down the spotless hallway but then she smelled something. 'Smoke?' she said to herself. She ran down the nearest stairwell and into the Janitor's room where the smoke detector map was. The map said the server and kitchen were on fire. Isabella panicked and pressed the fire alarm. But before she could, the school went into automatic lockdown mode. All doors slammed shut and locked. Isabella was panicking but then remembered the janitor had spare keys in a drawer somewhere. So she searched and searched but found nothing. Then suddenly sprinklers started going off and the power cut out. Isabelle went to check if the doors only locked from the outside.

Surprisingly Isabella was correct. She opened the door and went into the hallway. She saw people running around and screaming. She saw the animatronic hall monitors attacking some students. Isabella ran all the way to the rooftop and tried to put in the code on the keypad but it kept saying, 'Doors will automatically open in case of fire.'

Isabella punched the keypad, saying, 'There IS a fire!' She turned back to go downstairs and ran to the nearest door and started banging on it. 'Is anybody there? Please help!' she screamed. She looked through the window but the curtains were closed. Then the door opened revealing a whole classroom of students who weren't aware of what was happening. Isabella ran in.

'Why are you guys even here anyways?' asked Isabella.

'Because it's school? Plus it's just a stupid drill!' explained a student.

'No, it's real! And the robots are attacking the students.'

'Shouldn't we evacuate then?' asked another.

'Already tried,' sighed Isabella. She went to open the window, looked out, and saw normal life in the city. 'I guess it's only us.' She walked up to the rest of the students. 'Anyways, what's your names?'

*Richard. Molly. Helax. James. Jack. Leah. Mason. Caroline. Hope.*

'I heard maybe, like, two names there but alright,' joked Isabella as went to open the curtains and check the hallway. Just as she did that she realised. 'Wait! Does anybody have a phone?'

'I do,' said Mason.

'Great!' exclaimed Isabella. 'Call the fire brigade.'

Mason called them, explaining the situation and where the fire was. Just then Molly saw a group of people run by. They must've known where everyone was and started banging on the door.

'Isabella, let those people in!' yelled Molly. Isabella opened the door and a small group of people ran in. Then she noticed it was some people from her class. 'Are you guys okay?' asked Isabella.

'We're fine but we would've been better if somebody hadn't screamed,' pointed out Elizabeth.

'I'm sorry, again…' muttered Samuel. As soon as he finished talking the lights started buzzing and turned on.

'I guess that's an im-' Hope said before the whole building started shaking!

Isabella yelled, 'Get under a desk!' Everybody got under the nearest desk just in time for ceiling tiles to collapse. Isabella saw a bag next to her and decided to rummage in case there was a phone. Luckily she found one and dialled the nearest hospital and tried to explain what was happening.

The lady on the other end of the line said, 'Listen, I was a child too, but prank calling is very bad.'

'Wait! It's not a-' Isabella tried before the lady hung up. She crawled out from under the table and saw that the window that led to the hallway had broken while she had been calling. 'We need to move classrooms…' she muttered.

'No! This can't be happening! We're all going to die! No!' screamed Elizabeth.

'We're not going to die if you don't scream!' said Isabella.

'Don't tell me what to do!' screamed Elizabeth.

Isabella walked over to the door and slowly opened it.

Everybody slowly walked out of the classroom in a line and stayed near the wall. 'If we go down to the cafeteria we might burn, but if we go to the left we can go to the PTA donations room. That has food and a sink,' suggested Isabella.

'I think we should go left,' whispered Richard.

'Alright, make a signal to everyone.'

'We got in just in time…' exclaimed Hope. 'I saw a crowd of robots chasing us.'

Isabella didn't reply. She walked over to the shelves and looked around. 'Hey, there's a wall phone here,' she pointed out. 'Maybe it works.'

'No, it's ancient,' said Elizabeth, clearly disgusted.

Isabella ignored her and dialled 999 and pointed out that they had called and nobody had shown up.

'Of course Ma'am. We'll send as many ambulances and fire trucks as we can.'

'Thank you,' said Isabella then hung up. She walked to a window and saw lots of students running around. Just then the lights buzzed even more before going out.

'Ugh, not again. Wait… didn't the PTA donate flashlights?' pointed out Mason.

'Yeah, that's right… Start searching. Maybe we can shine the lights out the windows and bring in any survivors!' commanded Isabella as she began searching. But then more ceiling tiles and most of the shelves fell down due to the shaking. 'I think we should leave… Maybe if we grab something heavy and run fast enough we can break the glass doors at the entrance.'

'I agree,' said Mason.

Everyone grabbed something.

'Are you guys ready?' said Hope.

'Yup,' muttered everybody.

Hope opened the door and they all bolted to the stairs, every other survivor joining the crowd.

Everybody threw the things they found at the doors and tried to find their lockers. 'NOBODY HAS TRIED TO ATTACK US. WE HAVE TIME!' screamed Isabella as she bolted to the exit. Just two minutes had passed and everybody that was in the crowd had escaped. 'I can't believe that actually worked and nobody in the crowd even got hurt.'

As the crowd of students sat in the carpark the ambulances and fire trucks finally arrived and most people were whisked to safety.

# Teachers

Lucy

mr o'DaDDY

charlotte

**Charlotte O'Dowd**

# When I Was At School
## by Claire-Marie Taggart

When I was at school I was excited
To see my friends every day,
To wave hello to my teacher,
To learn and laugh and play.

When I was at school I loved music
And reading and counting and art,
Learning news words and lots of new facts,
Going home, feeling really smart.

When I was at school I felt special
When my teacher gave me a sticker,
When they smiled and praised my work each day,
When the books I could read got thicker.

When I was at school I loved lunchtime,
To eat my food on a tray,
To sit with my friends and talk nonsense,
Before we ran out to play.

When I was at school I felt empty
When my last day had finally come,
What was next, what would I do?
What kind of adult would I become?

When I was at school I told myself
I would be back one day,
To feel the way I felt before,
But have much more to say.

I'm back at school as a teacher,
I feel the excitement each day,
When my class wave at me fondly,
Before we laugh and learn and play.

I'm back at school as a teacher,
I watch the children progress,
I see them achieve their goals each day,
And it's me they want to impress.

I'm back at school as a teacher,
But nothing feels different to me,
I'm still the same girl, who's trying her best,
To be the best she can be.

I'm back at school as a teacher,
I'm part of an amazing team,
Surrounded by learning and laughter,
I'm living my childhood dream.

# Memories of
# St. Augustine's Primary School
## by Margaret-Maria Mullen
## (aka Mrs Elliott)

I started Primary 1, Room 1 on a sunny August day and I was full of enthusiasm. I had two older brothers at the school and I was desperate to know what this school business was all about. I had turned five years old in the March, I was so excited. I remember standing at the infant door with all the other new children and their mums, waiting to enter our classroom for the very first time. It didn't take long for me to realise that my new teacher who smiled and spoke kindly in front of my mum, was in fact just a wee bit scary. The parents were barely out of the door when her demeanour changed completely and I was petrified of her! I saw someone very like her later on in life when watching the movie *Matilda*! A clear memory of my first teacher was an incident that occurred due to my inability to get the straw in the strange triangular shaped milk cartons. I made the unforgiveable mistake of spilling some of the milk. I thought nothing of it; a paper towel will fix this surely? Little did I know this crime was indeed extremely serious in the eyes of the teacher. My punishment was one that was normal for the time but I won't go into it in case I scare the younger generation!

As luck would have it, ten of us were chosen to move into Room 2 to be with some children who were from the January intake of pupils. (There were two intakes at that time; we're not talking yesterday!) I settled into school life in Room 2 and all was going well. This teacher seemed slightly less scary but I was wary! The memory from this class was an incident with a 'chalk jotter'. This was a wee jotter with sugar paper and you took it home with a bit of chalk to do your sounds. Anyway, I had done my homework this particular night and had left my jotter on the table to put it in my bag the following day. The next morning, when I picked up the jotter, something wasn't quite right. It looked a bit worse for wear. I opened it with trepidation. I was right to be worried. Inside the jotter, all of my beautifully formed letters had been destroyed! My pest of a wee brother had got his hands on the jotter and the chalk. (I won't give his name but he can often be seen in Room 5!) Needless to say, I was upset. I remember my mum saying, 'Just explain to the teacher' and five-year-old me inwardly screaming, 'Are you joking? This woman is going to eat me alive!'

Now as it happens, she didn't look at everyone's jotter so I could be in luck. She held up Angela's jotter first. Oh dear, Angela's letters were not quite formed properly, she got a roasting! I could feel my anxiety levels going through the roof. She was walking about the class, she was saying my name, she was reaching for the jotter…It didn't end in me getting a sticker that's for sure. I never told my mum. Well, that's not true; I did tell my mum but I was in my twenties at the time! I do have a very happy memory of Room 2. I met my best friend in that class and we're still the best of friends until this day. It was a really foggy day and my mum was at the school to collect me. They asked if anyone else lived near us and my mum walked her home. The rest is history.

In due course I moved happily into Primary 2. This particular teacher's bugbear was pencils dropping on the floor. (No carpets in those days to soften the sound!) On one particular day we were sitting at our individual desks, all facing the front and the boy beside me dropped his pencil. There was a deathly hush, the teacher's head popped up like a meercat and she said those words we all came to dread, 'I heard a pencil dropping.' (Her hand cupped to her ear and her laser eyes scanning the room). When I think of it now I always hear the voice of the Child Catcher from *Chitty, Chitty, Bang, Bang*! Anyway, she located the culprit very quickly, probably because every child was pointing at him as they feared they might be blamed instead. Then I made a terrible error, I picked up his pencil for him and put it on his desk. Little did I know this was something he would be blamed for, for letting a girl pick up his pencil as well as the major crime of dropping it. Strange days indeed!

Primary 3 was the start of better, happier times at the school. This teacher was the kindest, most gentle woman I'd ever met; so nurturing, calm and quietly spoken. New teachers began to arrive at the school who came with a new way of working with children. I was content and flourishing at last.

My final 2 years at the school were my happiest there. I thought my new teacher in Primary 6, who I had for two years, was amazing with his platform shoes, brown flared trousers, and the big lapels on his jacket. (It was the late 70s after all!) He had lots of new ideas too, we learned lots of things about the world and even some French. I grew to love writing in his class, mainly because if you wrote a good story then you stayed in class to redraft it for the wall and didn't have to go to hymn singing in the GP Room! It was this teacher that made me want to be a teacher. An inspiring teacher, the one we all want to be to someone, and on occasion we're lucky enough to be told we have been. I loved my school and moving on, I was always proud to say I was a pupil of St. Augustine's Primary.

I'm now back in my second incarnation at St. Augustine's and in my seventh year as Depute Head Teacher here. At the end of June, I will have spent the same time working here that I did as a child playing and learning here. It's strange how things work out.

# The St. Augustine's Way
## By Linsay Platt

Quite often, I'll find myself casting my mind back to the 16th of August 2021 – my first day at St Augustine's Primary School, Coatbridge. I arrived at school early to a still and silent classroom – imagining what it would look like when it was busy, filled with the pupils of Room 15. Wondering what they looked like, what interests they had and – most scarily of all – what if they thought I was a terrible teacher?

Suddenly, as if no time at all had passed, the bell rang and the 2021-2022 school year was officially started. Glancing nervously out of the window into the top yard, I wondered which line of pupils were mine. (I had to ask Mrs Longyear on the way down the stairs because I was so nervous I had already forgotten.) The butterflies in my tummy had become elephants and suddenly all thoughts of the summer holidays had melted away in my brain like an ice cream during a heatwave. (Or an ice cream left in Room 15 – which seems to have a tropical climate of its own.)

As I made my way out to the top yard, I was met with a line of smiling faces staring back at me. Greeting them all with a 'Good Morning!', I was very quickly humbled with a reply from a voice from the back of the line asking, 'Why are you talking like a Primary One teacher?' So, that was me told. Every day is a school day - even for teachers.

One thing that struck me almost instantly was the kindness shown by the classroom full of brand new

Primary 6 pupils now sitting in front of me; offering to help hand things out, helping each other with their reading or solving a tricky problem in Numeracy. This kindness extended beyond the walls of the classroom and throughout the school building; from the pupils in the corridor saying hello or chatting to me about what topic they were learning about in class, to the Primary 2s and 3s holding doors open for me while I was carrying a heavy box up the (3!) flights of stairs to Room 15.

Even now as I write this, you've all grown a bit bigger and learned a little more, the kindness with which I was welcomed into the St. Augustine's community still shines through on a daily basis. Now, I have learned that kindness truly is the 'St. Augustine's Way' and how lucky I've been to be a part of that.

**Sitting Down 4 for I.C.T.**

(To be sung using a Jody Call)

Room ⑤ is the place 4 for me,
Sitting down for I.C.T.
We make monkeys happy and...
We program Scratch to OUR commands,

Little by little we're learning more,
Soon there will be other doors,
But room ⑤ was the place for me,
Sitting down 4 for I.C.T.

(Peace to all)

Kevin Mullen

You don't know what I am,
    I live under the stair,
There's no cause for alarm,
    I'll stay under the stair,
I'll do you no harm,
    Come closer and stare,
I grab your wee arm...
    Now you're under the stair.

Francis O'Dowd Snr

## Hymn to Saint Augustine

Hail thou first of doctors holy,
Vessel of election thou,
Once the slave of sin and error,
Saint of God, we hymn thee now.

Great Augustine, holy patron,
Grant that we may never stray,
From the righteous pathway leading,
Onward to eternal day.

Thine it was in times of danger,
When the power of hell was nigh,
 To defend  God's truth unchanging,
And its bitterest foes defy.

Great Augustine, holy patron,
Grant that we may knever stray,
From the righteous  pathway leading,
Onward to eternal day.

*Written by the teachers in the mid 1960s
(long before any of the current teachers
were born).*

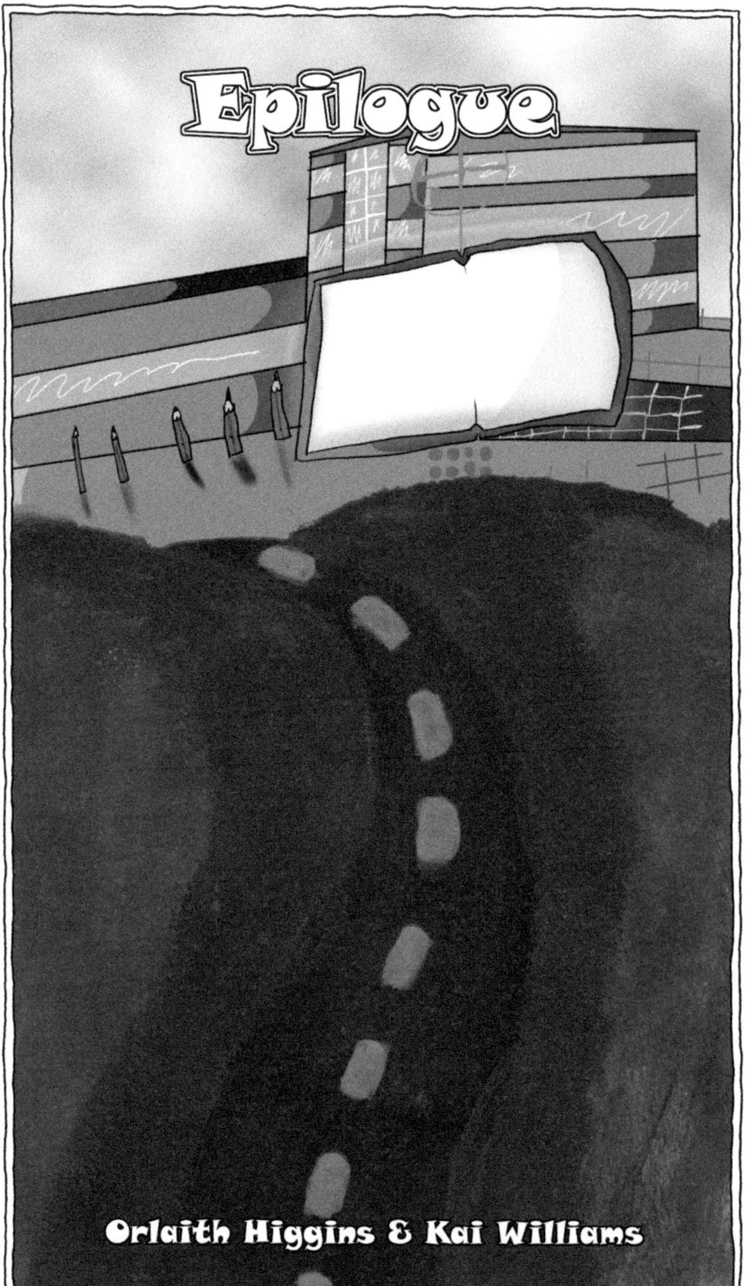
Epilogue
Orlaith Higgins & Kai Williams

# Gaudete
## by Connie Wilks

We hope you enjoyed our fabulous book,
We're happy that you chose to take a look.
When you picked up this book at the check out counter,
You had no idea the stories you'd encounter.

The stories are happy and full of joys,
Made by St Augustine's Primary,
The girls and the boys.

That you to all who helped in the making,
We are sure the future is yours for the taking!

are proud to present
a Few Words from
Our Sponsors
without whom this book would not have been possible.

# CANDY STORE
# WE HAVE IT ALL

Lanarkshires largest collection of sweets

Ice cream

Juice

Custom balloons

Cards for all occasions

Bus services available upon request for all events and trips

Key cutting deals

**AND MORE! COME IN STORE AND HAVE A LOOK!**

44 Whifflet Street 5am-10pm, seven days a week

Quadrant, Main Street 9-4 Mon-Fri, 9-2:30 Sat

# Yesterdays

## 47-49 Stirling Street Airdrie

Facebook - yesterdaysbarairdrie - Instagram

Monday Club 4 - 9 Karaoke

Frid - Sat - Sun Live Entertainment & Karaoke

Live Sports Everyday

# BRADY'S

## CRAFT BUTCHERS

YOUR FAVOURITE BUTCHER

**0141 375 9440**
**07857 662000**

**Being Catholic Television**

## Scotland's Catholic Television Channel

Broadcasting from 10am - 9:30pm every day

LIVE 10AM MASS

THE HOLY ROSARY, NOVENAS & DEVOTIONS

TALKS, REFLECTIONS & CATECHESIS

CHILDREN'S CORNER & TEENTOK

AND MUCH MORE...

VISIT: WWW.BEINGCATHOLIC.ORG

WATCH ON YOUR firetvstick

WATCH ON **Roku** TV

DOWNLOAD ON APP APPLE & ANDROID

# KAIROS
## CAFE

## Open Monday - Friday 10am - 2pm

### Serving hot and cold food and beverages

## ST. AUGUSTINE'S PARISH CENTRE.
## 12 DUNDYVAN ROAD, COATBRDIGE